NANCY WARREN

LACE AND LIES

VAMPIRE KNITTING CLUB
BOOK SEVEN

ISBN: ebook 978-1-928145-60-8

ISBN: print 978-1-928145-59-2

ISBN: hardcover 978-1-990210-31-0

Cover Design by Lou Harper of Cover Affair

Ambleside Publishing

INTRODUCTION

Cardinal Woolsey's Yarn Shop has been chosen to appear on TV which is great publicity – until a murder stops the cameras...

Celebrity knitting designer Teddy Lamont is coming to Cardinal Woolsey's knitting and yarn shop in Oxford to run a special class that will be televised.

Lucy Swift can't wait to host the popular, flamboyant designer and boost her business, but from the first day things go wrong. When a student is found dead, the publicity Lucy was hoping for turns out to be the wrong kind.

Lucy and her band of undead amateur sleuths must figure out who the killer is before her business winds up dead.

"Love this series...This plot is full of so many suspects that challenged me to really think about whodunnit although I always become so eager and engrossed that I forget to even try to figure it out, I just hunker down and let Lucy take me for a roller-coaster ride instead. Much more fun that way!" *Annette, reviewing Lace and Lies*

~

INTRODUCTION

The best way to keep up with new releases and special offers is to join Nancy's newsletter at NancyWarrenAuthor.com

LACE AND LIES

CHAPTER 1

"Teddy Lamont is coming to Cardinal Woolsey's." I was so excited I squeaked. Nineteen vampires stopped knitting, crocheting or gossiping to stare at me in various attitudes of awe. I'd saved the news until the vampires were meeting in the back room of my knitting shop so my grandmother would be among the first to hear it. I had wanted to watch her lined face beam with pleasure. And now I did.

Gran had started Cardinal Woolsey's knitting and yarn shop and, even though she was now undead, I still liked to include her in all business decisions. She'd agreed with my idea to offer our shop for a special promotion by Larch Wools. Larch was making a TV series featuring celebrity sweater designer and knitting expert, Teddy Lamont, who would teach one of his sweater patterns to a class inside a knitting shop.

Every knitting shop in the UK that carried Larch Wools had been invited to apply for the coveted spot. According to the letter I'd received, Cardinal Woolsey's was chosen for several reasons. We sold a lot of Larch Wools, Oxford was geographically in the middle of the UK, and the shop itself was photogenic and had room for a TV crew.

Several voices called out at once:

"When is it?"

"Can we all meet Teddy?"

"When will it be on the telly?"

I could only answer the first of these questions. "Filming takes place in a couple of weeks."

"So soon?" Sylvia spoke up. She'd been a silent film star in the 1920s, and based on starring in movies nearly a century ago, thought she knew everything about the entertainment industry. She looked me up and down critically. "You'll want to lose a few pounds, Lucy. The camera is unforgiving. And what will you wear? Hand-knitted items, of course, but of the highest possible quality."

All the vampires listened intently. Alfred, who'd never been a movie star but was as bossy as Sylvia, chimed in. "Yes. There's no time to waste. If we all get started now, we can have an entire television wardrobe for Lucy by the time shooting starts."

"I don't need a new wardrobe," I protested. My closets and drawers were already overflowing with hand-knitted garments from the vampires, who soothed their boredom by knitting me the most exquisite creations. The weight loss, however, was probably a good idea. Working in a knitting shop wasn't conducive to an active lifestyle. At least, that's what I told myself.

Sylvia eyed my long blond hair, which I'd stuck in a ponytail today since I was too lazy to style it. "You'll want to wear your hair back for the filming so the camera can see your face." She shook her head in fond reminiscence. "What a time I had of it playing Lady Godiva. Sir John Barrymore was beside himself trying to keep my face visible to the camera while preserving my modesty."

Normally, I loved Sylvia's trips down her cinematic memory lane, but today I was more interested in the upcoming televised knitting show than her long-ago triumphs.

"Who will be in your class, dear?" Gran asked, perhaps also feeling we should get back on track.

"The yarn company is choosing the students. They're running a national contest. Six lucky winners get to learn from Teddy Lamont. If they don't live within driving distance, they'll be put up at a hotel for the few days we're filming."

"My goodness. They're going all out."

I was both excited and nervous. In knitting terms, this was like having a movie star come to your house for dinner.

"How typical," Hester moaned. Hester was a hormone-challenged teenager whose awkward stage would last for eternity. I tried to feel sympathy for her, remembering the misery of my own teenage years, but she made it difficult. "Maybe I would have liked to be in the class, but oh, no. Everything gets decided by 'the man.'" She sighed theatrically and tossed the black shawl sweater she was knitting into her bag. Her entire color palette was black.

Sylvia laughed, and it was a bitter sound. "Darling girl, if it were possible for us to be filmed, I'd have played the dowager countess, Lady Grantham. I'm perfect for the part. Maggie, Judy, Helen, I'd give those Dames a run for their money. But we don't appear on film any more than we show up in mirrors or photographs. You can no more be a television or film star than you can sunbathe on the Riviera."

Hester's scowl deepened, and she kicked at her bag.

I felt so guilty. I'd never thought that my exciting news would be such a downer for the vampires who lived beneath my Oxford shop. "I'm so sorry," I said. "I didn't think. I can cancel it."

"Don't even think of such a thing," Gran cried. "This is wonderful publicity for Cardinal Woolsey's and for you."

"Maybe you can even learn to knit in the next two weeks," Hester said. When she was disappointed, she got mean.

I was trying to become a passable knitter even as I was

trying to become a better witch. But neither of those occupations were exactly easy. At least, not for me.

However, I hadn't completely wasted the business diploma I'd earned back home in Boston. I might be a fledgling witch and an inexperienced knitter, but I wasn't half bad at running a knitting shop.

The proof was that Larch Wools had chosen Cardinal Woolsey's to be featured on television.

I wondered who the six chosen knitters would be and whether Teddy Lamont would be as much fun in person as he appeared to be in his monthly magazine. I hoped so. Even his knitting patterns had personality. I was going to spend every spare minute of the next two weeks practicing my craft.

Both of them.

I'D NEVER HAD anything to do with television before, other than sitting in front of it and watching more episodes of *Grey's Anatomy* than were good for me. Meredith, Cristina and McDreamy got me through my breakup with Todd, and I'd forever be grateful. However, I'd never been involved with the making of a TV show, and I was a little starstruck at the very idea of a celebrity knitter coming to my shop and offering knitting lessons that would be televised. Needless to say, I was frantically trying to improve my basic knitting ability before all of the UK and wherever else this show would be broadcast noticed that the woman who owned the knitting shop couldn't knit. How embarrassing.

The director and producer of the show was Molly Larson. She was thirty or so, with long, sleek black hair and the kind of big smile that makes you want to join in, even when you don't get the joke. She swept into Cardinal Woolsey's with the kind of brisk efficiency that seemed to make even the balls of wool more energetic. She shook my hand, told me it was great to meet me and then wasted no time walking around my shop with a critical eye. I explained that I held my knitting classes in the back room and showed her, hoping quite desperately that none of the vampires were feeling sleepless in the middle of the day and likely to come up through the trapdoor. I'd warned them a hundred times not to do that, but they didn't always follow my rules.

"No, no," she said the second we walked into the back room. "We need the ambience of the front of the shop. It's not interesting enough back here." We both walked back out, and she soon had a plan to move all the displays in the center of the shop into the back room. "We only want one display of all Teddy's books, some of his magazines and a good stock of his knitting kits." She glanced around again, as though measuring for a rug. "We have six contestants. Do you have a nice antique table somewhere? I like the idea of the knitters sitting around one table, with Teddy standing at the head of it, demonstrating. Naturally, behind him we'll have a big display of Larch wools. What do you think?"

She seemed to require an answer, though I didn't really know why. Probably she just wanted my agreement. Well, I'd wanted this, hadn't I? So I was going to have to move some things around. It wouldn't kill me. "Why don't you come upstairs? That's where I live. There is a dining room table there. I think it might do."

She followed me upstairs. Nyx, my black cat familiar, was busily snoozing on the couch in the living room. She opened her golden eyes lazily and then, realizing I had company, raised her head to assess our new visitor.

Molly said, "Oh, a cat. How cute. So cute. Do you ever let it go into your shop?"

I couldn't have kept Nyx out if I'd tried. My cat tended to go wherever she felt like, and only a fool would try to stop her. Nyx yawned so wide, I worried she'd swallow her own head.

"Yes. She spends a lot of time in the front window. I've put a big basket of wool there, and she likes to curl up and sleep in the sunshine."

She made a note. "I love it. Love it! Getting your kitten snoozing in the front window will be one of our establishing shots. It immediately invites you in, suggests a cozy shop where a person could learn how to knit a tea cozy or a pair of warm winter gloves."

I could tell from the way she was talking this woman had never knit a stitch in her life. She thought a tea cozy was easy? Gloves? I'd like to see her try.

I led her to the dining table, which had been Gran's and probably her mother's before that. Molly turned up her nose at my table, shaking her head at the same time. "No. It's too fancy. I want rustic. I want oak or pine. Something scarred and solid. Scarred and solid. I want to give the idea of tradition. Of farm women sitting around knitting sweaters for their seven children or the wives of sailors at home around the table knitting to while away the time while their men were at sea."

I was somewhat puzzled. "But Teddy Lamont is all about fashion-forward knitting design. He's taken what was essentially a craft and turned it into art."

"You're right. You're right." I found that she tended to repeat the same word or phrase a lot. "He does. He does. But you see, what we're trying to do with this show is bring the two together. That's why we chose your shop. It's cozy and quaint, and it has a cat in the window. Then we bring Teddy and mix the old with the new. It's going to be great. Great."

I loved her enthusiasm, and if that meant I had to go find a beaten-up table from somewhere, I supposed I could do it. Rafe or Theodore would know where I could find one. But Molly was already on the phone. "Joseph. Good. Good. Glad I caught you. Come down to Cardinal Woolsey's shop right now. You've got to measure up and find me a table and the right chairs. Morgan will have to do something about the lighting."

Molly nodded again briskly, then hung up and turned to me. "I'm finished up here. If you can bring the cat down and put it in the basket, I can get the visual."

I glanced at Nyx, who stared right back at me. Nyx wasn't one to take orders from TV producers or to be hauled around like a prop. When she'd held my gaze long enough to make sure I understood this fact, she stood up on all fours, executed a perfect yoga stretch and then jumped nimbly down onto the floor. Tail in the air, she trotted down the stairs. When I opened the door into the shop, she wandered straight to the window, dipped her hind legs slightly and made a graceful leap up onto my window display. She climbed into the basket and curled up, posing with just her chin resting on the edge of the basket, looking back at us.

Molly was delighted. "She's gorgeous. Gorgeous! And so smart. You'd think she'd heard every word we said." Molly laughed heartily, and Nyx and I exchanged another glance. Then, clearly feeling she'd done enough to help me for one day, Nyx closed her eyes and drifted back to sleep.

"Good. Good. Joseph will take care of everything, don't worry. He'll source a rustic antique table and seven chairs. I want them all different. Different, right?"

"Right. Seven. Six contestants and a chair for Teddy."

She laughed. "Wait till you meet Teddy. He never sits. Absolutely never sits. No, the seventh chair is for you. You'll take the class, but really you're there to help any of the contestants who get tangled or confused."

"Tangled or confused." Now I was doing the repeating. What this woman didn't know was that I was the one most likely to get tangled and confused. "I thought I'd stay in the background, in case..." I petered out. I had no idea what I'd imagined I'd be doing, but it wasn't knitting.

In fact, if I was better at the other main activity in my life, being a witch, I might have been able to put a spell on this woman so she'd realize what a terrible idea it would be to put me on camera, but I'd had a couple of spectacular mishaps in the magic department recently, so I didn't like to mess with actual humans anymore, not if I could help it.

I soon discovered there was a lot more to making a simple television show than I could've imagined. Apart from the director and producer, there was a researcher, a camera operator, a sound recordist. I'd always wondered what a gaffer was when I'd seen the word on movie credits. It turned out the gaffer was the lighting tech. There was also a harried young woman who was the producer's assistant. She emailed me a lot with messages that began, "Molly thinks" or "Molly was wondering..." Still, it was exciting. After we closed on Friday, the TV crew were coming in and rearranging my shop and bringing in the table and chairs that they'd sourced.

Saturday morning very early, we'd get started and film all day. They were hoping to wrap it all up in three days, and I'd be open again on Wednesday.

I hesitated a bit about closing the shop, but my customers were so excited at the idea of Cardinal Woolsey's being on TV that business actually went up. I was easily going to make more money in the days leading up to the filming than I was going to lose being closed. Besides, since Teddy was launching a new book, *Lace My Way,* as a special treat for my customers and anyone who cared to drive to the neighborhood, he was going to do a book signing. We'd set this up in conjunction with Frogg's Books across the street.

Molly's assistant, Rebecca, who everyone referred to as Becks, sent me brief bios and photos of the six knitters who'd been chosen to take part in the show.

I scanned the list and photos, wondering if any of them were my customers. I recognized only one, Helen. They'd only given first names, but I knew her as Helen Radcliffe. She was in her mid-forties with short, iron-gray hair. She never wore makeup and dressed rather drably. She taught science at a local girls' school. She came across as quiet and intense and rather brilliant. She was a beautiful knitter, but she seemed terrified of color. My cousin, Violet, and I had both tried to expand her palette beyond shades often associated with small woodland animals, like rats, mice or muskrats, but it was hopeless.

I wondered what Teddy Lamont could do to encourage her to liven up her wardrobe, and I was excited that she'd been chosen. She needed to branch out from colors that could only be found in a mud puddle, and I thought he was exactly the man to give her the confidence to try.

I didn't know any of the other participants. Like knitting shops, knitters had applied to be on the show. The producers had obviously chosen people who were very different. If they were trying to say knitting wasn't just for little old ladies, I thought they'd succeeded.

There wasn't a single little old lady to be seen. A woman named Enid looked to be the oldest at around fifty. She was blond and very attractive. She lived in Stow-on-the-Wold, a Cotswold village about an hour's drive outside of Oxford. She was listed as a homemaker. There was a guy named Ryan who looked to be about thirty years old. His bio said he lived in Reading and worked in IT. Gunnar was a rugged-looking man originally from Norway, with close-cropped gray hair and a weather-beaten face. He'd been an engineer working on an oil rig in the North Sea. No wonder he looked so weather-beaten. He now lived in London.

Also from London was a very elegant young black woman named Annabel. She was a bond trader who knitted to relax from her high-stress job. Finally, there was Vinod, who was somewhere in his forties. He'd been born in India but had lived in Birmingham for most of his life. He was a radiologist by profession.

"Interesting bunch," a low male voice said, and I turned to find Rafe standing behind me and reading over my shoulder. I should have been used to it by now, but he still managed to surprise me, the way he could creep up so silently. He was wearing his usual outfit of dark trousers, though in deference to the summer, he wore a white linen shirt. He looked more than usually pale, since I was accustomed to seeing summer tans on most people in Oxford.

"Yes. They've obviously chosen these knitting students to prove that all kinds of people from all walks of life enjoy knitting."

He twinkled at me disturbingly. "Even the undead."

And speaking of the basement dwellers, I reminded him again of how absolutely important it was that none of the vampires come up through the trapdoor and into my back room during the filming or for a lot of hours before and after filming. There would be equipment and extra staff from the production company in there, and I didn't want to be responsible for either the heart attacks or the explanations when some poor, unsuspecting lighting technician found him- or herself face to face with a vampire.

"Don't worry. Everyone's been well warned. There are lots of other ways in and out of those tunnels, you know. We use this path most frequently, as we like to check on you."

That sounded kind and protective, and they were, but they were also bored and nosy and liked to know what was going on in the shop. Especially my undead grandmother, who used to own Cardinal Woolsey's and still liked to keep her hand in, cold as it was.

Nyx must have heard Rafe's voice, for she came over and twirled herself around his ankles, meowing piteously until he picked her up. She had a worse crush on him than I did. He lifted her up and hung her over his shoulder, one of her favorite places to rest, with her front paws hanging down his back and her head on his shoulder. As soon as she was settled, she began to purr loudly.

"She has you wrapped around her little paw," I said.

Rafe looked at me. "All the women in your family do."

CHAPTER 2

*H*onestly, having a bunch of vampires living below me was like having too many older, wiser relatives living in the basement suite. They were a bunch of know-it-alls, and even though I never thought any of them would revert to savagery and drain me of blood, I was always aware that they could. Frankly, I thought they used that knowledge against me.

However, they meant well, and they had been around a long time. Sylvia, Gran and Theodore all came up after Violet and I closed the shop. It was Thursday, and some of the film crew were coming the next day to prepare the shop for filming Saturday. I was hauling out the vacuum cleaner, worried about dust bunnies, but Sylvia and her cohort had decided some redecorating was in order.

"But Sylvia," I argued, "the producer said they chose Cardinal Woolsey's because it's so cute. Plus, there's an adorable cat in the window."

She shook her head, and her silver-white hair caught the light. "We have a rule in film. Never use livestock. They don't behave and cost a fortune in lost film time."

I immediately jumped to Nyx's defense. "Not my cat. She's special."

She made a noise not unlike something Nyx does when she's disgusted. Then she stood back and made her two hands into a frame, thumbs joined along the bottom and her fingers held together pointing up. She panned around the room, and we all watched her.

She stopped and said, "No. That poster has to go."

I'd become so used to that picture I'd stopped seeing it, but she was right. It was kind of faded and showed a field of sheep, with a hearty-looking couple in the foreground wearing identical highland sweaters. It was the antithesis of everything Teddy Lamont taught.

I didn't have time to go find another picture to put in its place. Gran pointed this fact out, but Theodore, who was very artistic and a set painter when he wasn't busy as a private investigator, said, "I could do something with these." He was inspecting a selection of antique knitting implements my grandmother had been collecting for years. They were in a display case against the back wall.

We all crowded around, and he said he'd paint a background and arrange and mount the whole display for me. I had to admit it would look a lot better than an old poster, and I knew he'd do a great job.

There was a short history of knitting and crochet in this cabinet and items of sentimental value, too. I'd bought Gran some of the antique pieces from the States as birthday and Christmas gifts. There was a Boye Needle Company crochet hook from the early 1900s, a nice pair of number seven steel double-pointed knitting needles, a sterling silver needle case and so on.

They directed me and Violet to move things around until they were satisfied, then they left us to do the boring cleaning.

Friday afternoon, I began moving things into the back

room. I said to Violet, "Let's put everything that's really heavy on top of the trap door so there are no surprises during filming." Naturally, the vampires would have no trouble moving anything heavy, but I thought the slight resistance might remind them that my shop was a Keep Out zone until filming was over.

Molly and Becks arrived, and within minutes I felt like I was on the set of a knitting shop rather than standing in an actual shop that sold wool. They hadn't been there very long, dropping terms like gimbal and data wrangler, when Becks grabbed Molly's arm. "Look, isn't that Teddy?"

We all turned as a small, wiry man came in the front door, setting the bells tinkling.

Teddy Lamont looked like a magical creature, and I knew magical creatures. He had twinkling blue eyes, an elfin face and the most incredibly restless energy. He seemed to prance from one spot to another as though he and gravity weren't on the best of terms. He had homes in San Francisco and in London, and his accent reflected that. He was enthusiastic about my shop and thought it was darling. I liked him immediately.

His life partner and manager, Douglas Tremaine, came with him, I thought partly to balance him. If Teddy was air and fire, then Douglas was earth and water. He was the knotted string that kept the helium balloon from flying off into space. Douglas was big and bearded with thick glasses and had somehow managed to pick up not a smidgen of a British accent. He sounded as though he'd just got off the plane from New Jersey, not that he'd been in London part-time for twenty years.

After Teddy had finished enthusing about the way I used baskets to display some of the woolens, which wasn't even my idea, Douglas said, "Don't worry, Lucy. He'll calm down." He gazed at Teddy with affection. "Eventually."

"Oh, don't mind him," Teddy said, waving his hand at the

big man as though he were a bad smell. "He wishes he had my eye for color."

"And you wish you had my eye for detail."

Teddy shook his head, as mischievous as an imp. "I'm just glad I have you for details. It allows me to be creative. Which is what I do best."

Molly and Becks were also wandering around my store. Molly looked up and said, "This is new." She pointed to the display of antique knitting and crochet implements that Theodore had hung up in the spot Sylvia directed him to. He'd painted a wooden board a muted gray-blue and attached all of the pieces with sticky backing in case I ever wanted to clean them or move them around. She walked closer. "What are all these things?"

I pointed out various knitting needles from different eras. She asked me a couple of questions, more I thought to keep me talking than that she was really interested. When I was finished, she turned to Becks. "Let's make sure and get a little snippet of Lucy talking about these antique knitting tools. We can use it as filler if we need to."

I wasn't thrilled at the idea of being singled out, but Gran would be pleased. Anything that highlighted me and the shop would be good for Cardinal Woolsey's reputation and business.

Naturally, we had all of Teddy Lamont's books, recent issues of his magazines and the pattern kits that Larch put together under his name. Even though I'd created a whole display, with some help from the neighbors downstairs, he wanted me to rearrange it all in a certain way. As he reminded me, he had an eye for color. I had no pretensions to being any kind of designer, so I was only too happy to rearrange the books until he was satisfied. I could tell from the way Molly and Becks treated him that they really wanted him happy. So did I. He was a rock star in the knitting world, and it was a great honor to have him here. I hoped, if this worked out, that he might consider doing another class in the future or another book signing.

I turned and out of the corner of my eye saw a woman with silver-blond hair sweep into the front entrance like a movie star stepping onto the stage. My heart sank down to the soles of my black sandals. I was convinced it was Sylvia, who missed the limelight as much as a 1920s movie star could whose face never showed up on film. I turned to make shooing motions at her when I realized it wasn't Sylvia.

The woman didn't even look like her. It was the way she carried herself and a certain theatricality in her movements that had made me think the person coming in the front door was one of my favorite vampires. I knew I'd never seen her before, but something about her was familiar. "Can I help you?"

She fluttered her hands around her face, and her gaze honed in on Teddy Lamont, too busy rearranging his books to notice. "Oh my goodness, no. I just wanted to get an idea of the lay of the land. I'm Enid Selfe, you know."

The name Enid was also vaguely familiar, and then the penny dropped. "Oh, you're one of the knitters who's coming for the class tomorrow. I'm Lucy."

"I was in the neighborhood. I couldn't pass your darling little shop without coming in to have a peek." She wore an elegant midnight-blue linen sheath, high heels, and a lot of jewelry that looked to my inexpert eye to be very expensive. Nobody got that dressed up to shop on Harrington Street.

She walked right past me and up to Teddy. "I can't believe my good fortune. You're Teddy Lamont."

"I am, dear lady." He took one of her hands between both of his. "And we're going to have the most wonderful time. Have you ever made lace before?"

She tittered. "Oh, not for years. I'm very rusty. And excited to learn from the best."

He was not immune to flattery. "You've come to the right

place." And then he winked so we could all think he wasn't that full of himself if we wanted to. "I hope you aren't one of those anal people who have to have everything perfect, though. The joy of my lace is that we make extra holes and boo-boos part of the beauty of the piece."

Overhearing those words, I swear I nearly wept. Here was a man who understood my kind of knitting. Since all the vampires had been knitting so long, they were perfect knitters without even trying. I felt as though new vistas were opening before my eyes. Vistas where I could knit for fun without always feeling like I wasn't good enough, my tension wasn't even enough, where it wouldn't matter if I didn't quite have as many stitches on my needle at the end of one row as I'd had before. When strange and wonderful designs took shape that bore no resemblance to the pattern I was supposed to be following. Were there others like me?

I'd liked Teddy immediately when I met him. Now I looked at him with new and probably worshipful eyes.

I would have tried to prevent Enid Selfe from monopolizing Teddy Lamont's attention, but just then, another woman came in. I was going to have to lock the door and put the closed sign up. The students could wait until tonight's book signing with a special reception to follow so they could all meet. But I realized that I did recognize this woman. She was one of my regular customers. Her name was Margot Dodeson. She was always meek and apologetic as though her coming into my store and giving me business was somehow an inconvenience to me. I had no idea of her age. She was somewhere between mid-forties and fifties. I thought she had once been pretty, but now she wore a disappointed expression. She looked like the kind of person who would rather fade into the background than ever be noticed.

"I hope I'm not interrupting?" she asked, hesitating with one foot in my shop and one foot still out on the sidewalk. I smiled at her reassuringly and went forward, holding the door so she could come all the way in.

"No, of course not. We're setting things up for tomorrow. You read my newsletter, I hope? Cardinal Woolsey's has been chosen to host Teddy Lamont for a knitting class. It's very exciting, though it does mean I'll be closed for a couple of extra days."

Behind me, I heard Enid Selfe still monopolizing Teddy Lamont. "Of course I'm coming to your book signing. Make sure you save a copy for me. I'm sure all the ladies will be lined up hoping for their special, personalized copy." She said the words with a kind of arch flattery as though she was flirting with him. Teddy Lamont couldn't be more gay if he turned up wearing rainbows and carrying a pride flag. I turned, wondering whether Enid Selfe was really that clueless. Or was she one of those people who just flirted with everybody?

Margot Dodeson followed my gaze. When she caught sight of Teddy, she put a hand to her chest and stepped back. "Oh my goodness." I thought she was going to turn and bolt out of the store.

I said, "Don't worry. Teddy Lamont is really very nice for a celebrity."

She shook her head. "If only I'd known, I'd have—"

I was desperate to put this poor woman at her ease. "I hope you're coming to his book signing tonight. He's giving a talk, and he's very entertaining."

Her color fluctuated between beet and snow. "A book signing. Oh, my. I hadn't thought—"

Behind me, Enid was telling Teddy how she'd taken his pattern for a Fair Isle sweater and made a few adjustments to the design. She sounded like one of those home cooks who review a recipe online and then describe how they've substituted every ingredient in the recipe for something else and how wonderfully it turned out, as though implying their cooking is better than the chef who put the recipe in the magazine in the first place.

Then she said, "We must swap phone numbers so you can text me if there are any changes to the schedule." She batted her lashes at him. "Or if you need anything."

She had her phone out and was looking at him expectantly. I saw him hesitate but his phone was sticking out of his pocket. Maybe he didn't want to alienate such an eager student before class even started. With some reluctance, he got out his phone and Enid texted him her number, then waited until he replied. She beamed. "That's lovely. And remember, you can call me anytime. Day or night."

Teddy must've made some sort of signal to Douglas, for suddenly the large man appeared at his side, and very deftly, as though transferring a knitting project from one hand to the other, Teddy passed Enid Selfe over to his friend and manager. I heard Douglas's deep booming voice ask Mrs. Selfe how she had come to be chosen as one of Teddy's students. She glanced wistfully after Teddy as he scampered away, rather like a rabbit escaping from a hunter. However, she seemed quite happy to talk about herself.

Teddy, meanwhile, made his way right over to us. He held out his hands to Margot and gave her his charming smile. "Are you another one of my students?"

She blushed back to beet. "Oh no. I only came because I ran out of wool for a sweater I'm knitting, and I knew that Lucy's shop would close for a few days."

He was still holding her hands. Now he brought them to his chest, against his heart. "My fault. Completely my fault. Now what can I do to make it up to you, since your favorite store is closed and all because of me?"

She blushed again and giggled. "No. It's not your fault. We're all very excited that Lucy's shop was chosen for the show."

"I tell you what. You come to the book signing tonight. I'll have something special for you. I can't tell you what it is. It's a surprise. Especially for you. What's your name?"

She told him, in a voice barely above a whisper, as though even to say her name aloud was being pushy.

Still holding her hand to his heart, he said, "Now, don't let me down. Promise? I'll be watching for you. And I will have a special surprise."

She nodded, and it was a little like a music fan finding out their favorite rock star had promised to write them a song. With a quick glance at Enid, who was still monopolizing his partner, Teddy whispered to me that he'd meet Douglas back at the hotel and quietly left the shop.

Enid was now saying, "I really needed this class. I've been so down. I'm getting divorced, you know."

"I'm very sorry," Douglas muttered politely.

Enid Selfe sighed, a loud, pathetic sound. "You'd think I'd learn, but I'm too trusting, you see. Men take advantage and then leave me brokenhearted and alone, after I've given them everything." She put a hand to his wrist and said, "And I do mean everything."

"This isn't your first divorce, then?" he asked, very much a man from California.

"Sadly, no. This will be my third."

He made a noncommittal sound and began to look longingly toward the door where Teddy had disappeared.

"I know what you're thinking, and you're right. I'm too naïve. Too trusting. It's my curse. However, I still believe my Prince Charming is out there." She batted her eyelashes at him. "Somewhere."

Poor Margot Dodeson was so flustered by Teddy's attention that she couldn't remember what wool she wanted. Luckily, I kept records in my computer, so it was easy to figure out what she needed.

As she was leaving, she whispered to me, "Of course, I won't come to the book signing. I'm sure he was only joking."

I hadn't known Teddy Lamont for very long, but I didn't think he would ever joke about his business. No doubt he was anxious to make sure he had a good crowd. "I'm sure he did mean it. You should come. It's over at Frogg's Books, and it should be a good evening."

"I don't know. I'll have to think about it."

"All the TV people will be there and the students. It would be nice for them to meet some of my regular customers." I pressed one of the brochures in her hands as a reminder and then said goodbye.

Then, feeling a bit like a martyr headed for some horrible punishment, I turned to relieve Douglas from Enid Selfe's attentions. She was telling him how her third husband had left her after unfairly accusing her of mental cruelty. She held a lace handkerchief to the edge of her eye as though a tear might fall, but I doubted she'd dare cry with all that makeup on her face. The damage would be enormous.

I forced a pleasant smile to my face and said, "I'm so sorry to interrupt, but Douglas, Teddy asked that you meet him at the hotel. I believe he wants to go over the evening's itinerary with you."

Douglas's look of gratitude was so intense I had to stifle a giggle. "Then I must go. My master awaits." And with a quick wave to both of us, he left the shop. Molly and Becks left in his wake.

Enid glanced around, and seeing only me left, she ditched the helpless, wronged woman role. She put her dry handkerchief back into her handbag and said, "Well, this is a nice little shop you have here. Now, how will the seating work for the filming?"

When I told her it wasn't up to me, she tried to find out where Teddy would be sitting and where the cameras would be set up. She was so clearly angling for the best spot that I knew if I was in charge of the seating I'd have done anything, including lying, to get her as far away from Teddy and the cameras as I could.

However, it wasn't my choice, and I truthfully didn't know how Molly planned to arrange everyone. I suspected that part of tonight's meet and greet was for her to see how the students interacted with each other and probably how they all looked together. No doubt she'd arrange us all in a way that worked best visually.

Unlike Enid, I hoped to be in the most camera-unfriendly position.

CHAPTER 3

rogg's Books was what every bookstore should be. Not too big, with staff who genuinely loved books, lots of comfy corners for settling down to read, and events with authors. Charlie Wright and Alice Robinson worked together in the shop, and they made a perfect team. Charlie was a slightly vague bibliophile who could tell a customer the proper order of the most obscure fantasy series, while not being able to remember where he'd left his tea. Alice preferred Austen to Tolkien, Sophie Kinsella to George R.R. Martin and could be relied upon to remember customers' names and where the books they'd ordered could be found.

Their romance had been very one-sided, with Alice worshipping her gorgeous but emotionally clueless boss for years until he'd almost lost her. Then, finally realizing the treasure under his nose, he'd smartened up and asked her to marry him. It hadn't been the most romantic proposal, as he'd been a murder suspect at the time, but Alice hadn't let a little thing like impending criminal charges stop her from accepting. Talk about true love.

Now, his name was cleared and they were as happy as a

Valentine's Day card. My assistant and fellow witch, Violet, and I had nudged the romance along with a touch of magic that nearly went horribly wrong, so I was really happy things had worked out. Since our shops were only across the street from each other, and Alice sometimes taught knitting classes for me, we were friendly. I was pleased that Charlie was hosting an evening with Teddy Lamont. I was hoping that he'd gain some of my customers, knitters who liked to read, and I'd gain some of his, readers who liked to knit and crochet. Even if there wasn't much crossover business, it was nice for me not to be responsible for this event or to have to arrange the catering, book orders and the cleaning up once the evening was over.

Naturally, I arrived early for the book signing. I'd left Becks supervising a team of people who were moving in a table and chairs, taping down cables on the floor and pretty much taking over every square inch of Cardinal Woolsey's. Nyx had given the whole operation one disgusted look and bolted. Recalling what Sylvia had said about working with animals, I hoped she'd be back tomorrow for her close-up.

I found Charlie settled in the chair behind the cash desk with his nose buried in a book. When I greeted him, he looked up and said, "Lucy. Wonderful to see you. This is a fascinating book." He held up Teddy's newest, *Lace My Way.* "I never knew there was so much that went into knitting lace. Or knitting anything else, for that matter."

He was nothing if not an eclectic reader.

"Yes. I'm looking forward to his talk tonight. Any idea how many people you're expecting?"

He blinked as though he'd forgotten he was hosting a talk this evening and then said, "You'll have to ask Alice. She's got all that under control. She's arranging chairs in the back."

Like Cardinal Woolsey's, Frogg's Books had a back area where they kept the less popular books, and there was a large, open space suitable for author talks. I thanked him and headed back.

Alice was well-organized as always. She had about thirty chairs set up, and there were still a couple of couches at the back for overflow, as well as some standing room, if it came to that. A podium and screen were set up for Teddy, and there was a long table with a good stack of his most recent book on lace as well as stacks of his older books for sale.

She was just placing a jug of water and a glass on the podium when I walked in. Alice had blossomed in the time I'd known her. She'd always been attractive, with long, red hair and the kind of clear, fine skin that seems particularly English. However, she'd come into her own in the last few months.

We hugged a greeting, but before I could ask how many people were expected tonight, Alice grabbed my shoulders and jumped up and down, squealing, "You won't believe it."

Alice wasn't the jumping, squealing type, so I knew something momentous had happened. Fortunately, her eyes were glowing and her cheeks were flushed in a good way, so I figured it was something good.

"What is it?"

"We've set a date for the wedding!"

I felt as excited as a witch whose love potion worked can feel. Alice and Charlie were wonderful people who belonged together, so it was natural that I began jumping up and down and squealing too. Our arms were on each other's shoulders, and sheer happiness kept us going until we were breathless. Then we pulled apart, laughing. "Tell me everything," I said, slightly hoarse thanks to the squealing.

"It's going to be a garden wedding."

"Lovely," I said. Given the usual wet weather in the British Isles, this was a brave choice.

"Charlie wanted to have it on the grounds of Cardinal College, since it's his old college, but..." She made a face, and I nodded. She didn't have to explain her reluctance to get married at the college. Bad things had happened there in the course of their slightly rocky courtship.

"I thought maybe the shop, as that's where we met and fell in love, but Charlie thinks it's too associated with work. We were at a standstill until Rafe offered to host the wedding at his manor house."

I felt warm and fuzzy that Rafe was doing something so nice. He'd become a lot less reclusive in the last few months and seemed to be trying to fit in with humans better. Still, this was seriously generous. He wouldn't be able to control who was invited, and Rafe guarded his privacy the way billionaires guard their billions.

"He and Charlie know each other, of course, through the book business. They're both involved with Cardinal College, and both are Friends of the Bodleian, but still, it's incredibly generous. You know how beautiful his home is. I could never have dreamed of having such a beautiful spot for my wedding."

"That's great. When's the big day?"

"The fifth of August. We're having the wedding on the Monday when both our shops are closed." She took a deep breath and clasped her hands together. "Lucy, will you be in my bridal party?"

I was thrilled to be asked and quite surprised. "Of course I will. I'd be honored."

She hugged me. "You gave me the courage to believe I could end up with Charlie, and I did. You're as special to me as a sister."

I felt my eyes mist. "I feel the same."

"Good, then it's settled." She pressed the tasteful diamond solitaire on her ring finger as though for good luck, then turned to practical matters. "Tonight's looking to be a very busy evening. I think we'll have a full house. At least forty people."

Teddy Lamont probably could have filled a much larger

space for his book signing, but the show producers had wanted to keep the intimate vibe going, and Frogg's Books was both intimate and visually appealing.

Enid Selfe walked in with a gorgeous young black woman I identified as Annabel, the London bond trader who was also in the class. They didn't seem comfortable with each other, more as though they had arrived at the same time and were being polite.

I also wanted to be polite, so I walked forward just in time to hear Enid say to Annabel, "You speak such good English. Were you born here?"

It was one of those moments when I wished that I had walked the other way so I hadn't overheard that appalling comment, and then swiftly tried to formulate a forgetting spell so I could delete this awkward moment from time. However, before I could do that, Annabel said, "I was born in London. And so were my parents, but my grandparents came over from Jamaica. They were ever so grateful to the British government for everything you did for them." Sometimes British sarcasm slides right by me, but this time I was fairly certain she'd said the words with a broad hint of irony.

Enid didn't catch it. She gave what could only be termed a condescending smile and said, "Oh yes, I know all about the Windrush generation. My third husband, Horace Crisfield, was with the immigration department. It was shocking how many people snuck into this country without proper papers, not even a passport. Of course, they had to be sent home. It was only right."

I hadn't lived in the UK long, but I'd heard about the Windrush scandal. After WWII, a number of Jamaicans had come to the UK when the 1948 nationality act gave commonwealth citizens the right to settle in the UK. Many arrived on a ship called Windrush. They lived in the UK and assimilated. They'd had children, bought homes, built businesses. In an immigration crackdown from 2009 to 2018, the government had begun deporting people who didn't have passports or the papers to prove they'd arrived legally. Some of those deported had left Jamaica as babies and never been back. The government backed down in the wake of massive public outrage, but not before lives had been ruined, sometimes irretrievably. The glance Annabel sent to the former Mrs. Crisfield was not a friendly one. *Forgetting spell. Forgetting spell.* Trust me to forget the spell I really needed right now.

"What did you say your husband's name was?"

"Horace Crisfield."

I thought Annabel was about to say more, but a gorgeous guy about her own age arrived. She must have recognized him from his photo, as I did. "You must be Ryan."

"Yeah. And you're Annabel." He chuckled. "This is a bit like an online date."

I wanted to introduce myself, but Annabel took the excuse to turn her back on us, leaving me with Enid.

I tried to make small talk with Enid, but she spent the whole time looking over my shoulder to see if there was someone more interesting to talk to. Oh, I hoped she found someone and soon. I wanted to like the students, but I found that I was taking a strong dislike to Enid Selfe.

As more people arrived, I wished someone would come and rescue me the same way that Ryan had rescued Annabel, when to my relief, Enid suddenly said, "Oh good," in a voice like a purr. Quickly she slipped a compact out of her handbag and checked her appearance and then, with a practiced efficiency, swiped her lips with lipstick in a gold case that I recognized as Dior and far beyond my budget. A pretty enamel canister followed, and she spritzed her neck with perfume.

Once she'd freshened her appearance and made me sneeze when some of her perfume went up my nose, she said, "Excuse me, Lucy. I've just spotted an old friend." What she really meant was, "Excuse me, Lucy. I've just seen someone more interesting to talk to than you."

As rude as she was, I was relieved, except that it was probably Teddy Lamont or Douglas she was beelining for and somebody would have to go and rescue them. Probably me.

I followed her progress and then realized it wasn't Teddy Lamont or Douglas who had caused the very female reaction. In fact, I was having the same reaction myself. Rafe Crosyer had just entered the room. He was tall, dark, and commanding. As a vampire, he naturally had the reputation of being cold, bloodsucking and predatory, but from the determined way Enid Selfe was threading her way toward him, I thought he had some competition.

He was taller than nearly everyone there, and his eyes scanned the room as though looking for someone. Then his gaze met mine, and I had the pleasant thrill of realizing it had been me he'd been looking for. His gray-blue eyes lightened, and he took a step toward me. Only one step, however, before Enid moved to cut him off. He looked slightly surprised at the interruption and gazed down at her.

It was fascinating to watch the way that woman who'd looked bored and barely present when I was speaking to her was suddenly transformed into a woman of charm and wit. I heard a tinkle of silvery laughter and, to my surprise, instead of finding an excuse to slip away from her, Rafe actually seemed to find her conversation interesting. To my shock, I saw her raise her perfectly manicured hand and touch his chest as though to emphasize whatever fascinating thing she'd just said. Rafe's chuckle was low and deep, and it took a long time for her to move her hand off his chest.

Not wanting to be caught staring, I turned to find Margot Dodeson standing at my elbow. She was also looking over at Rafe. He did draw the eye. I pulled my gaze away with an effort. "Margot. I'm so glad you came."

"I wasn't sure, but he did specially invite me." She glanced over at Teddy, who'd just come in and was already surrounded. "Maybe it was a bad idea."

"No. He'll be so pleased."

She nodded, looking unsure. Fortunately, Charlie came up. She must shop here as well. "Margot. Pleasure to see you. I know this is meant to be a knitting evening, but there's a new historical novelist you might like. She's a cross between Hilary Mantel and Margaret Atwood." Wow, I thought, that was some cross. Margot looked thrilled that Charlie knew her and obviously knew her reading tastes. He led her away to the front part of the shop.

"Don't be late for the talk," I warned them. Charlie would forget they were hosting an author evening if he got caught up with literary chitchat.

Margot said, "Don't worry. I'll come back."

Rafe wandered up, and I said, "You seem to have made a new friend."

He glanced back at Enid, who was now talking to a prosperous-looking older gentleman whose wife was perusing Teddy's latest. "Reacquainted with an old friend, in fact. She's a Friend of the Bodleian."

"Ha. I don't think it's the Bodleian she's interested in befriending."

"I beg your pardon?"

"Rafe. She was hitting on you."

He looked down his long nose at me. "It does happen, you know."

"But she's so much older than you are."

"Actually, I'm several hundred years older than she."

"But—do you like her?"

"I find her quite charming. And she knows a great deal about Egyptian history, which is one of my interests."

No wonder the woman had married so many times. She

obviously had something that she could turn on for men or, I thought unkindly, maybe only rich, eligible men, and Rafe was certainly one of those, if you discounted his eating disorder and the whole undead thing.

I needed to get my head around this. "But do you like her, like her?"

When he was teasing me, he had a way of looking very serious, but there was always a disturbing twinkle in his eye. He had it now. "Currently, my romantic interest lies elsewhere."

Naturally, that made me blush and realize—not for the first time—that he had several hundred more years' experience at flirtation, relationships and love than I did.

I said, "Well, I don't like her."

He looked over at Enid, who was now talking to Teddy, and then back at me. "I suspect she may be one of those people who doesn't waste her charm or attention unless she believes it will bring her some return."

I was thankful that he could see through the woman. I didn't own the man, and in spite of our attraction, I was nervous about getting involved with a vampire. Still, I didn't want him getting caught up with someone like Enid.

Before I could say more, Rafe said softly, "Bubble, bubble, toil and trouble." I followed his gaze, but his words had already telegraphed who would be coming in. Sure enough, while it wasn't the twisted sisters of *Macbeth*, it was three witches—my cousin Violet, my great-aunt Lavinia, and the head of our coven, Margaret Twigg. Violet was my shop assistant and probably believed she was my mentor, but in truth she was more likely to drag me into trouble than help me learn my magic. She was a superb knitter, though, and for that reason alone I was happy to have her working at Cardinal Woolsey's. Also, it was nice to have someone working in the shop who wouldn't freak out if flames accidentally started shooting out of my fingertips. Not that that happened so much anymore. I was learning control, but since my magic was more innate than learned, I still screwed up.

Margaret Twigg was probably more of a classic mentor. She was a very powerful witch, and she had helped me in the past, but she could be very sarcastic, I didn't think she liked me, and frankly, I was pretty wary around her.

All three women were rather exotic both in appearance and clothing choices. Violet had long black hair with ribbons of pink and purple dyed at the front, framing her face. Margaret Twigg had a head full of corkscrew curls, piercing blue eyes and red lips that seemed permanently curved in a knowing smile. She looked a bit like Vivien Leigh in *Gone with the Wind,* if Vivien had lived to be very old and was a witch.

They greeted me with nods, but I could tell they were more interested in making new friends. The two older witches went straight up to the crowd that was hanging on Teddy Lamont's every word, while Violet headed toward Alice. From the corner of my eye, I could see that Alice was also sharing her good news with Violet. They didn't do quite as much squealing and jumping up and down, but it was pretty clear that Violet was very happy to see this love story enjoy a happy ending. As she should, since the love potion she'd initiated had nearly had disastrous effects.

I was sorry that my grandmother couldn't be here, especially seeing my great-aunt Lavinia, her sister, mingle with the other guests. But Gran was too new a vampire. It would be decades before she could show her face again in Oxford without freaking people out. Still, I knew she'd be waiting anxiously to hear all about the evening when I got home.

Violet and Alice were still chattering away. I turned back to Rafe. "That's so kind of you to let Alice and Charlie have their wedding at your home."

"I think so, too."

CHAPTER 4

*B*ehind the three exotic witches came a woman who suddenly seemed remarkable for her very drabness. Helen Radcliffe looked as though she'd been through the wash too many times. Or had spent years working underground. Her short, gray hair looked as though she might've cut it herself while she wasn't wearing her glasses. As usual, she didn't have a speck of makeup on, and she wore a pale gray hand-knit cardigan over a washed-out gray T-shirt, a pair of old and faded blue jeans, and sneakers that were more about comfort than fashion.

Since Helen didn't seem to know anyone, I took it upon myself to greet her and then introduce both of us to Annabel and Ryan, her fellow students who seemed to be the friendliest.

"Are you nervous?" Ryan asked. "I think I am. My girlfriend entered me as a joke. I never would've done it on my own."

Helen smiled and glanced at me. "Lucy encouraged me to put in the application. I don't think it would have occurred to me. But it will be exciting to learn how to make lace, and Lucy and Violet are always encouraging me to try a bit of color. I don't know. I'm never sure what color works with what, so it's easier to stick with the neutrals."

I thought that calling that sad gray sweater neutral was giving it too much credit. "But I'm not nervous, no. I'm a teacher so I'm used to an audience."

"Really?" Annabel asked. "What do you teach?"

Helen pushed her glasses up her nose. "Science. I taught for years at a private school that was full of very bright girls. But because the parents were paying a great deal for their children's education, the scrutiny was intense. It got to be too much for me. So I took a year's break. I've just begun a new job at the local public school. I think that will suit me better."

Two men walked in together. One was burly and rugged-looking with a weather-beaten face, his gray hair shaved close to his head. I recognized him right away from his photograph. His name was Gunnar, and he'd worked at sea on oil rigs. According to his profile, he had taken up knitting while quitting smoking. He was Norwegian. With him was Vinod, the radiologist who'd been born in India but moved to Birmingham when he was a child. They both paused in the doorway and looked around.

When Vinod spotted me, a smile broke out onto his face, and he came forward, holding his hands out. "Lucy Swift, I presume?" he asked in a Brummie accent. "I read all about you on your website."

I smiled back. "And you're Vinod. I read all about you on your profile."

"I'm delighted to meet you in person. It's very exciting, isn't it? Knitting on camera."

Exciting wasn't the word that sprang immediately to my mind. Terrifying, nerve-racking, holy heck how was I going to get out of it? Those were the terms I came up with when I contemplated the upcoming show.

He glanced around eagerly. "And where are the other victims?"

Now he and I were talking the same language. But he said it with a wink as though he weren't serious. I pointed out Annabel and Ryan, who were chatting together like old friends, including Helen in their conversation, though she seemed quite happy to just stand there and listen to them. Helen seemed more than usually nervous. She kept glancing over her shoulder, and her hands were shaking. I hoped it wouldn't detract from her knitting, since I was the one who had encouraged her to apply for this thing. I wanted her to embrace color, not end up in a padded cell, heavily medicated.

Meanwhile, two cameras were setting up. Vinod went to join Ryan, Annabel, and Helen, motioning Gunnar to join them. Rafe came over to me and said softly, "I didn't realize this evening was going to be televised. I'll slip out."

I nodded, completely understanding that he didn't want to show up as an empty seat when the camera panned over the audience. "I'll catch up with you later."

It was nearly time to begin, and Teddy Lamont gracefully extracted himself from the eager group around him and began making his way to the podium. He stopped and cried out, "Dear lady, there are you are!"

I glanced around, and I think everyone else did to see who had elicited this cry of delight. It was Margot Dodeson. She was holding a Frogg's Books bag, so obviously she'd taken Charlie's advice and decided to give the new historical author a try.

She blushed and backed away, even as Teddy rushed toward her. "I'm so glad you came. I've been looking for you. I told you I had a special gift, and I do."

"Oh, you didn't have to." She glanced around as though checking for escape routes. "I was just happy to be invited."

But he grabbed her hand and dragged her toward the podium.

"You come this way." Naturally, the camera was recording all of this. I almost wondered if he had chosen Margot because she was so shy and unused to being the center of attention. There was nothing rehearsed about this. From a canvas bag with one of his designs on it, he withdrew what looked like a paperback version of his latest book. "Do you know what this is?" he asked her.

She looked worried, as though this might be a trick question. "It's your book."

"Yes, but it's a proof copy of my book. It's got mistakes and boo-boos in it. One day, this will be a collector's item. Well, you can hock it tomorrow on eBay and make a few bucks, but I hope you won't." We all laughed, and she shook her head, blushing furiously. "I would never."

And he wrote something in the flyleaf with a flourish and handed her the book. She backed away, looking equal parts mortified and thrilled.

TEDDY WAS NOT a man who hid behind a podium. He used it to put things on while he moved around, gesturing to the slides he put up on screen, asking questions of people in the audience. Always active. I had watched him before, as he had some video segments of himself teaching on his website, so I knew what to expect. He was engaging, funny, and he made lace knitting sound exciting and approachable.

But more than anything else, he talked about color. At heart and by training, Teddy Lamont was an artist. He'd begun as a painter but then began to marry visual arts with crafts, such as quilting, needlepoint and knitting. He'd done more than anyone I could think of in the recent past to make these ancient crafts fashionable. I didn't think that someone like Annabel, a fashion-forward London-based bond trader, would have taken up knitting if it weren't for designers like Teddy.

I felt strangely proud, as though just by hosting this televised class in my shop, I was doing my bit to bring these beautiful and relaxing handcrafts into a mass-produced, overscheduled world.

When he finished, there was resounding applause, and a nice long lineup formed to get signed copies of his book. Naturally, most of the students and I lined up too. Teddy had a personal moment and funny line or two for each person who had their books signed. When it came my turn, he twinkled at me. "It's Lucy, isn't it?"

"Yes, but I wonder if I could have it signed to someone else? Could you please make it out to Agnes? She's a dear friend, but she couldn't make it tonight."

This wasn't an unusual request. All he said was, "Tell Agnes she missed a great show."

I laughed. "She did." And how my dear Gran would've loved to be here.

I stayed a few more minutes to be polite, but we all had to be at the shop early the next morning, and so I headed across the street and home.

I didn't even bother going upstairs to my flat but headed straight into the back room of the shop and down the trapdoor, using one of the flashlights I kept handy. I guided myself along the dark tunnel until I reached the sturdy oak door where Gran and some of the vampires lived. I rapped the special knock, and Gran herself open the door. Her face suffused with delight when she saw me. "Lucy, I was hoping you'd come."

Gran had begun dressing much more stylishly since she'd become a vampire. Mostly, I thought, under Sylvia's influence. Probably since they spent so much time together, Sylvia wanted her companion to be as well-dressed as she was herself. Gran wore black linen slacks, a silky cream-colored shell and Chanel flats on her feet. However, the cardigan she was wearing was pure Gran. It was made of nubby blue wool and was a triumph of comfort over style.

She led me into the sitting room, where Rafe and Sylvia were discussing a real estate purchase. They closed the computer when they saw me, and Rafe rose to his feet. He was such a gentleman, he always did that when a woman entered the room. He came forward and brushed his lips against my cheek. "I was waiting for you to text me. I'd have escorted you here. How did it go this evening?"

My cheek tingled where he kissed me, but I tried to keep my thoughts on knitting. "Fine. In fact, it was fabulous."

I handed the book to Gran, and her reaction was everything I could've hoped. She clutched it to her as though giving the book a hug. "Oh Lucy. What a wonderful thing to do."

"He signed it to you," I told her. She opened the flyleaf and sighed the way, in her youth, she might have mooned over a picture of Clark Gable. She read aloud, "To Agnes, remember: Lace is like dreams made real. The lace never lies. With love from Teddy Lamont."

"What a wonderful quotation," she said, turning to me. "Where did it come from?"

"I think he made it up. It's in the introduction of his book, and he used it in his slideshow without attributing the phrase to anyone else."

"Well, he's a poet as well as an artist. He's right, too. Perhaps that's why we're so drawn to lace. It's as gossamer as a dream, as weightless as a wish—"

"And as complicated as a faulty Rubik's Cube," I finished.

Gran laughed but shook her head. "Lucy, all you lack is practice."

"And desire," Sylvia added. "Until you want to be a really fine knitter, you never will be."

She was right, of course. To me, knitting was a chore and an obligation rather than the pleasure it was to true knitters.

Frankly, I felt the same about my witchcraft. I was a bit scared of it, and if I could've passed on my "gift" to a more deserving witch, I happily would have. Still, fate had handed me both innate witch powers and a knitting shop. I pretty much had to figure out how to make both of them work.

"Are you excited about the class tomorrow?" Gran asked me.

"Yes, as long as I can keep the camera away from my work."

I was sure Sylvia was about to remind me that I was the least important one when Hester wandered in, yawning. She rubbed her eyes and looked cranky. "What did I miss?" She was always convinced that the best conversations, activities, and the best part of life happened when she was not there to witness it. I doubted that was true, but there was something about Hester that made me not want to include her in everything I did. No doubt the vampires felt the same.

"Nothing, dear," Gran said. She was always nice and patient with Hester. "Lucy was just telling us about Teddy Lamont's talk. She brought me a book. You can look at it if you like."

Hester glanced at the book and slumped onto the couch cushions. "No thanks."

Then she looked sideways at Gran. "I'm going out soon. Can I have some money?"

Gran's forehead creased, and she glanced at Sylvia and Rafe before answering. "What's happened to your allowance?"

The vampire teen made a sound like a verbal flounce. "That pittance? It's barely enough to keep me in makeup."

It was Rafe who spoke up now. "Hester, what have you been doing?"

She looked like a teenager who'd been caught out doing wrong, which I supposed she was, even though this teenager was several hundred years old and should surely know better. "Nothing. You need to increase my allowance. You treat me like a child."

He didn't make the obvious response that she was acting like a child. Instead, he said, "I'm going to walk Lucy home now. We'll talk about it when I get back."

She crossed her arms over her chest and glared. "You're not my dad."

"Thank heaven for small mercies."

He stepped toward me and held out his hand. "Shall we?"

Even though I was perfectly capable of walking the short distance between the vampires' lair and my shop, Rafe always liked to escort me. He said there were other, less friendly creatures about, and I knew it was true, but so far I'd never met any.

When we got up to my shop, we both hesitated. I was thinking about inviting him up to my flat but didn't want him to get the wrong idea, and he seemed equally reluctant to end our time together. Finally, he said, "Would you like to go for a walk?"

It was getting late, but I knew for him this was like morning, and he was always more comfortable after dark. "Yes, I would," I said. It was July and the day had been very warm, but I knew the night could get cool, so I grabbed a sweater, and we headed out into the night. He clicked open his car, and I laughed. "You invited me for a walk."

"I did, but I don't want to walk around Oxford. Let's get out into the country and look at the stars."

"All right."

We didn't have to drive far out of Oxford to get into the country, and I imagined no one knew the area better than Rafe, who'd been intimate with the hills and valleys for half a millennium.

It was peaceful driving along in the silent Tesla. I told him about Teddy's talk, and soon he was pulling off down a country road. To my surprise, he reached into the back seat and lifted out a picnic basket, a beautiful wicker one with leather straps that looked like it had come from a fancy shop. "You planned this."

"I thought you could use some relaxation before you start the busyness tomorrow. We won't stay long, don't worry. You'll get your rest."

I didn't feel a bit tired but thrillingly alive, being out here in the dark with a man who was never more alive than when the rest of the world was sleeping. He led the way along a narrow trail that wound through old trees and then out into an open clearing. We were up on a hill, and it was such a clear night, as I looked up I saw countless stars and the beautiful silver crescent of a first quarter moon.

Rafe opened the basket and removed a red and black plaid blanket, which he shook out and laid on the grass at my feet. I was charmed and slipped off my shoes before settling myself on the warm blanket. He brought out a bottle of red wine, a plate of cheese and bread, some smoked salmon and grapes. There were little pots of dip and gourmet crackers.

"This looks amazing," I said, popping a grape into my mouth. He poured each of us a glass of the rich red wine.

"I can't take credit for anything but the idea. William did it all."

William Thresher was Rafe's butler, chef and friend. I knew he found preparing Rafe's meals less than exciting and always claimed to be thrilled when he had humans to cook for.

I was happy to be the recipient of his genius in the kitchen. I'd bet he'd made the dips and maybe even the bread himself.

We settled back. I knew the basics of stargazing. I could recognize the Big Dipper, and the North Star, but Rafe pointed out Cassiopeia and Hercules.

It seemed very natural to curl up against him and rest my head on his chest. As I gazed up and saw millions of stars twinkling down, most of which he could name, I said, "We're awfully insignificant, aren't we?"

"Yes."

He turned to me, and his eyes gleamed in the darkness. He kissed me and then said, "Lucy, what am I going to do with you?"

"I don't know, but you can do that again."

CHAPTER 5

$\mathcal{T}$he first day of filming started really well. In spite of my late night, I woke early. Nyx was on my bed, one paw over her eye, so she looked like a pirate wearing an eye patch. "If you can be that cute all day, our show will be a guaranteed hit." She blinked the one eye at me.

I decided she was promising to be adorable and kissed her on top of her black head. I showered and spent extra time doing my hair so it hung in soft ringlets around my face. Sylvia had already consulted on my wardrobe choices—not that I'd asked her to. I'd vetoed a couple of her suggestions, and she'd shut me down too. Finally, we agreed on a cream-colored summer skirt and, obviously, a hand-knitted top. It was mint green and as thin as gauze, though it wasn't lace, because that would have looked rude and as though I were trying to show off. I hadn't knitted the top myself, of course. Gran had, which made me happy. As the weather was warm, it was nice to be able to wear something that was both hand-knitted and cool.

Everyone arrived early and appeared to be in good spirits. Teddy was so full of energy, I thought the cameraman might have a hard time keeping him in focus.

The students were allowed to sit wherever they liked, and the younger people naturally gravitated to sitting together, while the older ones settled closer to Teddy. Enid Selfe had arrived first and claimed the seat nearest the teacher. Teddy looked less than thrilled, and Molly pursed her lips but didn't say anything.

Once again, Enid had dressed up. I suspected from the perfection of her makeup and hair that she'd visited a salon this morning. Her dress today was red, very eye- and camera-catching, and over it she'd wrapped a hand-knitted shawl in black.

A lace shawl.

This woman needed lessons in how to knit lace the way I needed lessons on how to eat chocolate.

Helen arrived next and I was so happy to see a familiar face and a woman I knew well. She was wearing a linen dress that was the color of mushrooms and a sweater the color of moss, if the moss had been dead for some time. She blinked at all the changes in the shop and all the people and equipment filling the small space. She glanced over at the table where Enid was already monopolizing Teddy and instead of joining her, walked over to the new display.

"This looks wonderful, Lucy." I would have to tell Theodore of the compliment. "I remember my grandmother knitting with needles just like these," she said. "I still have some of her old knitting patterns. Probably her wool, too."

I suspected she did and was still knitting sweaters with the old, faded wool from decades ago. This woman seriously needed a knitting intervention.

Then Ryan and Annabel arrived and I went to greet them. Even as everyone greeted each other with friendliness and good will, I experienced the first niggle of dread.

I, naturally, as the teacher's helper, *gulp*, sat at the foot of the table, while Teddy stood at its head. Behind him was a brag wall of Larch wools, his kits and his books. He wore a royal blue linen shirt that made his eyes shine like a couple of mischievous sapphires, faded blue jeans and soft brown leather loafers. He had one of his own hand-knitted sweaters tied around his neck as though it was giving him a hug.

Molly let everyone sit where they liked. In front of every student was a Larch Wools bag, and everyone had been told not to peek. This provided a birthday party atmosphere. Presents! Whatever was inside the bags was a surprise.

Molly came forward and instructed us not to look at the cameras or they'd have to edit that out, and it was a lot of work to do so. They wanted us to follow Teddy's directions, knit, chat when there was a break and, most of all, have fun! This was fun!

I only hoped the cameras stayed far from my handiwork. When I'd moaned of my fears to Sylvia, she'd assured me the cameras weren't going to follow my knitting. This was about the students learning from Teddy. "You'll be there almost like the furniture. You own the shop. You're young and pretty, and you're part of the story that knitting isn't for old ladies. But you're not part of the lesson, so if you don't draw attention to yourself, they won't waste a lot of film on you." She sounded so confident that I felt immediately reassured, even though the last time she'd been on film, her costar had been Rudolph Valentino.

Molly handed the floor to Teddy, and he immediately beamed at all of us students as though being here was the greatest delight he could imagine. Before he could say a word, Enid said, chiding, "Teddy, you naughty man. You didn't call me. I was all ready to make you lunch. I'm a very good cook."

His good mood dimmed as though his battery was running low. Helen looked hurt. "You gave Enid your private number?"

He wrestled with himself for a second then said, "Yes. And we should all have each other's numbers. This shooting

45

schedule is intense and you need to keep knitting when the cameras are off. If you're really stuck on something, you can text me."

"That's so kind of you," Helen said, immediately looking happier, especially since Enid was now scowling. She wasn't so special anymore.

Everyone's belongings were in the back room so Teddy went and retrieved his phone. He tapped away then said, "I've made a group. Add your name and mobile number. I'll delete the group when this is over." He glanced at Enid as he said it.

Once that was done, he returned his phone to the back room and came out again.

He looked at Molly who said, "Remember, class, you keep your eyes on Teddy, each other and your knitting. And one, two, three, action."

"Good Morning, class," Teddy said, smiling and opening his arms wide as though giving us a collective hug.

It was hard not to smile back with so much impish goodwill coming at us. He talked briefly about lace knitting and, naturally, referenced his new book. Then, he said, "You can open your surprise packages now."

Honestly, a bunch of kids at Christmas couldn't have ripped into the bags any faster than this group of adult knitters.

Annabel gave a cry of delight as a rainbow of wools spilled out onto the table in front of her. Teddy chuckled. Every bag contained a range of colors, but each was different.

"Look at those colors!" He went up on his heels and down a few times, not jumping, exactly, but not far off. "I don't want any of you to be afraid to experiment. Lace is traditional. Knitting is traditional, but we don't have to be. We're going to push the boundaries."

Enid spoke up sharply. "I don't believe lace is meant to have its boundaries pushed."

There was a tiny pause, and then Teddy continued, "When you think of lace, what do you think of?"

Before Enid could voice an opinion, he pointed at Annabel. She said, "Weddings."

He nodded. Pointed at Ryan. "My gran used to edge fancy pillows with lace."

"Right. We think of lace as staid and stodgy." Teddy shot a glance at Enid's black lace shawl, and Helen giggled softly. Hopefully too softly to be picked up on microphone.

"Lace is also the last refuge of the perfectionist," Teddy continued. He waved his hand in the air. "I say to heck with perfectionism. It holds us back. Let it go. Get in touch with your creative side. The part of you that's bold and wants to experiment with color and form and shape and texture. Be a kid again. Crayon outside the lines."

Enid might be hating every second of this, and from her pursed lips and sour expression, she was, but oh, he was speaking my language. Someone who believed in color over perfectionism? Finally, I'd found my knitting guru.

"I've been knitting for years. Love it. But here's a secret. Nothing I do is perfect. Nothing." He lifted an item that had been on a lower table behind him. It was a gorgeous lace square. "This is a cushion cover. Isn't it gorgeous?"

It was. It was Moroccan-looking with reds and oranges and yellows and threads of gold. He waited for the coos of admiration to die down and then turned the piece over. "Now look at the back."

Seriously, in that moment I fell in love with Teddy Lamont. The back of his work looked familiar. It looked a lot like mine.

I loved that he'd made all his boo-boos and messes part of the creation. I felt myself relax as I looked at all the colors on the table in front of me, the blues and violets and reds and one yellow. I imagined they were crayons and I had a basic design in front of me with encouragement to make it my own. As Teddy said, to color outside the lines.

But not everyone wanted to color outside the lines. I glanced at Enid Selfe and watched her poke through her colors as though she were picking through weeds, looking for a flower. I felt reluctantly sorry for her. It was pretty obvious she'd come here to be the class show-off. The teacher's pet who sits at the front and drinks in praise. She was clearly an expert lace knitter, but she was out of her element when asked to play with color and not bother about perfect stitches.

She was discovering, within half an hour of the class beginning, that she wasn't going to be the best. She was the embodiment of everything Teddy Lamont wanted us to change. She did not appear excited at the notion of trying new things.

Enid managed to keep quiet while Teddy taught the basics of the lace stitch. I discovered that when I wasn't so frightened about getting everything wrong, I was able to relax, and that made everything go better. My tension wasn't as tight. I didn't feel like the knitting needles were my enemies. It was sort of fun.

We were all doing cushions, so the piece was a basic square. However, each of us had a distinct palette of colors, and while Teddy had provided the basic design, he really encouraged us to play. Maybe if we weren't all aware this would be on television, we wouldn't have been very daring, but knowing that knitters across England would be watching spurred us all on to try harder.

Ryan was doing something that looked vaguely like hot-air balloons. He'd sketched out a simple idea with his palette of primary colors, and I was instantly jealous that he'd thought of something so wonderful. I thought I'd honor my witch heritage by doing a version of a pentagram. I had an idea that I could make it with all these different colors and it would be silky and soft and lacy. But the hot-air balloons looked much more sensible.

After an hour, Teddy announced that he needed a coffee break. Everyone began to put down their knitting, and Molly rushed up and said, "No, no. You have to keep knitting. We'll come back when you've got an inch or two knitted and talk about how you're doing in your design ideas, and Teddy will come around individually to each of you. But you have to keep going."

That seemed fair, and I thought poor Teddy needed a break. I'd told Molly and Becks about Elderflower next door and warned the sisters who ran it to expect a lot of TV people coming in to grab coffees and sandwiches.

Once he left, we began to chat amongst ourselves.

"I want to make my daughter a little lace sweater to wear when she starts university next year," Enid said to us all. "She's going to Oxford, of course. Or Cambridge. We haven't decided yet." She smiled at us all condescendingly. "She's clever enough and well-rounded enough that she can get in anywhere. I made sure of it."

Helen glanced at the woman with dislike and muttered, "She'll look a fine sight wearing a cushion to Oxford."

I tried not to laugh, but Vinod looked at Helen and grinned. "Poor Oxford," he whispered.

"That's a beautiful sweater you're wearing, Gunnar," Helen said. "Who taught you to knit?"

He seemed surprised to be addressed, but he answered readily enough. "It was the cook on my rig in the North Sea. I was trying to stop smoking but not so easily. I tried chewing gum, but I needed to fill my hands with something." His hands were big and work-roughened, and it was easy to imagine him smoking. Also working with the thick wool and blues, grays and white that I associated with Norwegian knits like the one he was wearing. They weren't delicate, and neither was Gunnar.

However, he'd been given a lot of greens, oranges and purples and was sketching out some ideas, not ready to commit to knitting his lace yet.

I was always interested in how people had learned to knit, and it was good market research for my shop, so I followed Helen's lead and turned to Ryan sitting at my right and asked him who taught him. Before he could answer, Annabel said, "I bet it was your mum or your grandma. It's usually the older women who pass down the love of knitting. It was my granny who taught me when Mum was at work."

Ryan nodded. "You're right. My grandma taught me. She's Jamaican." He said the words matter-of-factly, but I think we all stopped knitting to stare. Finally, Annabel said, "You're part Jamaican?"

Ryan looked up and grinned at her obvious surprise. "No. I'm adopted."

Enid Selfe overheard the conversation and asked him when his birthday was. In some surprise he said, "July 30, 1990."

She smiled at him. "Have you ever found your birth mother?"

I began to feel uncomfortable, and I thought Ryan looked very much so. "No. My parents are my parents. I wouldn't want to hurt their feelings."

She put down her knitting and counted on her fingers, then nodded. "You could probably be my child. The timing is about right. I had to give a baby up, you know," she said as though it were an everyday occurrence. "I was far too young to bring up a child on my own. It was a boy, I think."

Who had a baby and didn't even know whether it was a boy or girl? Ryan's jaw bulged as though he was clenching his teeth, and then he asked, "Did you ever try and find the baby?"

"No. I've always thought one day I'll probably come across

him. Or her." She put down her knitting and rose. "I'm well ahead of the rest of you. I think I'll go next door and get a decent cup of coffee."

When she'd left, Annabel leaned toward Ryan. "Looks like you might've found your mommy dearest."

He rolled his eyes. "If that woman turned out to be my mother, I'd have to kill myself. Or her."

CHAPTER 6

*T*he next morning I arrived at the shop early, which was not that hard to do considering I lived above Cardinal Woolsey's. I wanted to make sure everything was tidy and all the chairs arranged properly before the film crew arrived, before the students arrived, and most definitely before Teddy Lamont arrived. After getting off to such a bad start yesterday, I hoped he was still going to show up.

Things had started to such great promise. How had one woman derailed our class so thoroughly and so effectively? I felt guilty as though this was somehow my fault, when all I'd done was provide the venue. I hadn't chosen the class participants. Still, I didn't like the fact that my knitting shop was even vaguely associated with someone as unpleasant as Enid Selfe.

She'd made yesterday a nightmare. She'd argued with him, called his work substandard. She'd corrected the other students. Finally, an hour before we were scheduled to finish the class, she'd interrupted him again, and he'd thrown down his own work and snapped, "Maybe you should teach this class."

Instead of being shamed, she nodded. "At least I can knit lace properly."

And Teddy Lamont had walked out.

I'D SLEPT BADLY, so badly that I'd clearly heard somebody moving around late last night downstairs. If Cardinal Woolsey's was a normal shop and I was a normal woman, I would've called the police. But with a nest of vampires living below, many of whom liked to spend a few of their nighttime hours knitting, at Cardinal Woolsey's we'd taken late-night shopping to new heights. The vampires came and went as they pleased and helped themselves to whatever they wanted from the shop, but they were very good about writing down what they had taken, and every one of them paid their bills on time. I wished all my customers were as conscientious.

I came down the stairs, fresh, strong coffee in my hand, hoping to caffeinate myself awake. I opened the connecting door between my flat and the shop. It was seven o'clock in the morning. The film crew were due to arrive in an hour, and class participants another hour after that, so I had some time to make sure everything was nice and tidy. I hoped I'd get the chance to catch up on some emails and see if I'd received any online orders, which I always tried to mail out quickly.

After that awful class had ended yesterday, Molly had asked Enid to stay behind. Molly had a key to the shop, so I left her to it, going out with everyone else instead of upstairs to my flat. I didn't want them to know I lived up there in case they all came up to complain. I'd gone across the street and whined to Alice, who was a very sympathetic listener.

I hoped Molly had dealt with Enid and talked Teddy into coming back today. Teddy was a professional, and I was certain he'd show up. I half-hoped that Enid wouldn't. In the meantime, I had mail orders to sort out.

That's what I was thinking about, packing and mailing balls of wool and knitting kits to places around the corner and as far away as Australia and China, when I saw her.

Well, that's not exactly true. First I struck my toe on her. I thought for a moment when my toe hit something solid that I'd stubbed it on some spare equipment or a prop left behind by the film crew. I looked down. Enid Selfe was lying there.

She was staring up at me, at least that was what it looked like in the early morning light seeping in from the front window. She was lying on her back, staring up at me out of sightless eyes. Enid Selfe would never disrupt a knitting class again.

Enid Selfe was dead.

I didn't know I'd dropped the coffee until I felt the scald as the hot liquid splashed my legs.

Things seemed to happen out of order. I felt the burning, then I heard the coffee mug hit the ground. Then I became aware that a pool of coffee was soaking the dead woman's clothes and that I had just contaminated a crime scene. It was impossible to even separate the jumble of my thoughts and the way I saw and heard and felt and even smelled the catastrophe.

The smells of coffee and death mingled and threatened to gag me. I rushed to the door. I needed fresh air if I was to stop myself from heaving. Just as I moved to grab the door handle, I realized how stupid I was being. I'd already dropped coffee all over a dead woman. I was not about to mess up the forensics any more.

So I pulled myself together as best I could and backed away from the door, noting as I did so that it appeared to be unlocked. I saw no obvious signs of forced entry, not that I was any expert, of course.

Had I forgotten to lock the door? With all the expensive

camera equipment in here? No. I was positive I hadn't. And even if I had forgotten to lock the door, why had Enid Selfe returned? The day was over, we had said goodbye, and even she must've realized she wasn't the most popular of the knitters. Molly wouldn't have left her in the shop. Would she?

I had to call the police. I glanced over at her again, knowing I had to make absolutely sure she was dead. If there was any life at all, maybe it wasn't too late to save her.

I flipped on the overhead lights. I didn't want to, death was easier to bear in the dark.

I walked back over and forced myself to look down at her once more. The eyes were open, staring up as though she was furious with the ceiling. She had an angry look on her face, and her lips were pursed as though she was about to argue. She actually looked exactly the way she had when she'd been arguing with Teddy Lamont about the correct way to knit lace.

He'd looked angry enough to kill, but then I think everyone around that table had felt the same way. People got killed for crazy reasons all the time, but surely this woman hadn't been killed over a knitting stitch?

It was only now that I realized what she'd been killed with. One of those sharp steel knitting needles that Theodore had displayed on the shop wall had been driven into her chest like an ice pick. Its mate entered her chest from the other side, the way you'd stick two needles into a ball of wool.

Still, I had to check, and so I got to my knees and lifted her wrist, feeling for a pulse. She was stiff. The term *rigor mortis* went through my head, and with a shudder I let go of her wrist and wiped my fingers on my skirt.

I called the police emergency line and told them what I'd found. They told me to stay where I was and someone would be right over. It was a good thing the 999 operator told me to stay with the body, because I seriously wanted to run very far and very fast away from here.

I was going to have to open the door anyway in order to let the police in—that was my justification for opening the front door. I knew that if I didn't get some air, I might seriously embarrass myself by throwing up. I'd already tossed my coffee all over the poor woman. I didn't want to toss my cookies as well.

I found an old tea towel that I used sometimes to dust the shelves. It was a souvenir from the Tower of London but so old the tower had faded to pale gray in places and there was a hole in one corner. Carefully, I used it to open the door.

I screamed when something black flew past me and jumped a mile in the air. That's how rattled I was. I didn't even recognize my own cat.

"Nyx. You shouldn't be in here," I scolded, though I'd never been so happy to see anything or anyone in all of my life. With the true instinct of a curious cat, she immediately padded over to Enid. Nyx leaned her nose toward the dead woman and back again several times, so she looked as though she was dabbing something on the dead woman's face. She turned, and those gold eyes stared at me as though saying, "Lucy, really? Another dead body?"

Even though she hadn't spoken, I answered her. "It's not like I want these things to happen. I don't kill people, you know."

She seemed to understand that I needed all the comfort I could get right now. She walked around me, rubbing her lithe body against my ankles, now sticky with coffee. I leaned down and picked her up, and she crawled up and over my shoulder, hanging there, heavy and warm and comforting. She didn't purr. I suspected it was out of respect for the dead. Or maybe my jangly nerves were too much for her.

While I waited for the police, I started to call Molly, the producer. She needed to know what was going on, and hopefully she could stop the film crew from arriving. I hoped she could also prevent the people who were supposed to be in the classroom from showing up. But, then I thought maybe the police would want everyone to show up. To see if someone didn't. Someone who might have blood on their hands.

So I put my phone away. I couldn't think clearly anyway. I'd wait for the police, and they could take over from here. All I wanted to do was go upstairs, crawl back into bed and put the covers over my head. Maybe book a flight back to Boston.

One-way.

I'd never seen a dead body in my life until I'd arrived in Oxford. Now I seemed to stumble over them all the time.

It's because you're a witch. The words lodged themselves silently in my head.

Had the thought come from Nyx? In case it had, I spoke aloud. "You don't know that. There are thousands of witches in the world. They don't attract death to them. Most are healers and people who understand the world in a way most mortals don't. I'm the only one I know who seems to draw corpses the way a picnic draws flies."

The ambulance arrived first. And close behind that was a police car with lights flashing but no siren. Fortunately, it was still early in the morning, and no one was in our little street shopping. After I'd told them how I'd found her, a uniformed cop asked me to wait upstairs, which I was more than happy to do. I apologized about the coffee, and Nyx and I went back upstairs.

I poured myself another cup of coffee, and then when the smell hit me, I couldn't drink it. I threw the dark liquid down the sink. Instead, I brewed some calming herbal tea. I added a healthy shot of Cotswolds honey for comfort. I sat on the couch, and Nyx crawled up in my lap. My hands were shaking so hard, the cup rattled against my teeth, but the tea definitely helped. I closed my eyes and tried to calm myself. Nyx began to purr then, low, rumbling, soothing sounds that picked up the rhythm of my own breathing and seemed to slow it down until I felt the calm creep over me.

When the knock came on the door, I was ready.

I ran downstairs to open the connecting door and found Detective Inspector Ian Chisholm standing on the other side. I'd known Ian almost as long as I'd been in Oxford. We'd even dated a couple of times. There was a slight hesitation between us now, as I think both of us tried not to remember that awkward interlude.

"Lucy," he said. "Are you all right?"

I would've liked to be one of those women who could come back with a smart, snappy quote in times of stress, but the truth was, I could barely get words out at all. I just nodded and stood back to let him in. A uniformed officer came up behind him.

When he came upstairs, Ian just looked at me with his eyebrows slightly raised. He didn't have to say anything. This wasn't the first time a dead body had been found in my shop.

The silence stretched, and I giggled nervously. "We'll have to stop meeting like this."

He nodded. "Tell us what happened?"

I didn't even know where to start. Finally, I explained about the television show and the students being chosen, and then I told him that Enid had been one of them.

"So you never met her before this television show?"

"That's right. She came into my shop the day before filming started. Teddy Lamont was there, and I think she was hoping to meet him." I thought about telling them how pushy and annoying she'd been, but I didn't want to assassinate her character, not when someone had already assassinated her. In a strange way, I felt protective of the poor woman. She was dead. I didn't want to start talking trash about her.

"So, she came to meet Teddy Lamont. And then when did you see her again?"

"Well, all the students were invited to Teddy's book signing that night at Frogg's Books."

"Did she arrive alone? Was she with anyone?"

I had to think back. "I think she was alone." The way she was hitting on the few men there, I certainly hoped she was alone.

"Did you see what time she left? Or who she left with?"

I shook my head. "I left before the other students."

I forced myself to hold my gaze steady and not let myself blush. I didn't want Ian to know that I had snuck out early to meet my vampire grandmother. Instead, I said, "I had a big day coming up yesterday. I wanted to make sure I got a good night's sleep and had everything ready when the filming started."

I thought that sounded very reasonable and probably what I would've done if I hadn't been out stargazing with a vampire.

Ian seemed to accept my story. "And filming started yesterday, you said, for this television show?"

"Yes."

"Did anything happen? Did Enid Selfe seem upset or frightened? Worried about anything?"

"No." Quite the opposite. She'd caused upset rather than felt it.

"The whole day was filmed?"

"Yes."

Ian would obviously ask to see all the footage from yesterday's lesson, so I thought I'd best own up about some of the behavior I had witnessed so I didn't look suspicious. I chose my words carefully. "I think Enid Selfe could be the kind of person who made enemies."

His eyebrows rose at that, and his green eyes peered at me intently. "What makes you say that?"

"You'll want to watch all the footage from yesterday's filming. Enid was rather opinionated about her knitting. I don't think she appreciated Teddy Lamont's style. It's very relaxed and casual, and she struck me as quite a perfectionist."

He looked to me like I might be slightly nuts. "Are you suggesting that woman was murdered because someone didn't like her knitting stitches?"

"I'm not suggesting anything, but you may have noticed she was murdered with knitting needles."

"That was hard to miss. As was the puddle of coffee dropped beside the victim."

CHAPTER 7

I felt my face grow hot in embarrassment. "I'm so sorry. That was me. It was the shock. I literally walked right into her, and then I looked down and saw her, and the coffee just fell out of my hand."

He nodded. "Could happen to anyone. Does rather mess up my crime scene though."

"I am so sorry." I felt like telling him dropped coffee and a dead body weren't doing much for my business either.

"As you say, we'll be looking at all the footage from yesterday, but give me the highlights. Tell me about the other students. Did any of them seem particularly antagonistic towards the victim?"

It would be easier to say which of them *weren't* antagonistic toward Enid Selfe.

In anticipation of the police asking me questions about the class in my shop, I had printed off the pictures and bios I had for each student. I handed them to Ian and then glanced at the clock on the wall. "I didn't tell the producer about the murder. I was going to, but I thought you might want all the students to show up as though the class were going ahead."

He glanced up from his reading, paused. "Yes. That's a good idea, Lucy. We not only want to see who does show up but, even more important, who doesn't."

I hoped my good thinking made up a bit for me slopping coffee all over the dead woman, but I wasn't sure I completely evened the score. I supposed it would depend on what forensics were still able to glean.

As though he were thinking the same thing, Ian said, "You didn't touch anything else, did you? Like the needles in her chest?"

I shook my head. *Eeww.* "The only thing I did was check her pulse. I was fairly certain she was dead but had to be sure."

"Fair enough. Wrist or throat?"

I shuddered at the very idea of touching that woman. "Wrist." I could still remember the clammy, cool feel of her flesh beneath my trembling fingers.

He went back to reading the printout. When he'd finished, he looked up. "All of these people are knitters?" He sounded shocked.

"That's the point of this program, I think, to showcase an assortment of people who all knit. Get away from clichés."

Teddy and the knitting class were due at my shop at ten. When I reminded Ian of that and the fact that I hadn't phoned Molly yet, he passed me back the pages with the bios of the students. "Forensics will be busy downstairs for some time yet. Is there somewhere else nearby where you could hold the class?"

I thought about it. There was the church hall at the top of the road, but it was a big, rather uninteresting room. Besides, it was Sunday. There would likely be activities going on. I walked to my window as though looking out on Harrington Street might give me inspiration, and of course it did. There, right across the road, was Frogg's Books.

Charlie didn't open Sundays during the summer. The

students had been there once. They wouldn't think it was strange to meet there again. I suggested this to Ian, and he agreed it was a good idea.

"But you have to get rid of all these police vehicles and the ambulance, or it will tip everyone off that some disaster's happened."

He glanced at his watch. "Call the producer. Put them off for an hour. Make sure you can get into Frogg's Books. In the meantime, I'll get all the emergency vehicles moved. The team will still be busy in here, but you shouldn't see anything from the street."

"And you'll come up to Frogg's Books and tell everyone what's happened?" I didn't want to be stuck with that horrible job.

"Yes, I will. Make them comfortable. Give them tea or coffee or something, and I'll arrive about half past eleven."

"I'll have to tell Molly. She's the producer. It's her job to change the venue."

He appeared to find this news rather inconvenient. "Ask Molly to meet you at the bookstore earlier than everyone else. Tell her there's a problem but don't tell her what it is. First thing we need to do is make sure she shows up."

"Molly? You think the show producer might've murdered one of the cast of her own show?"

He gave me a disdainful cop to layperson glance. "At this point in the investigation, everyone is a suspect."

The way he said everyone with that emphasis suggested he thought I might be a suspect too. Great. Exactly what I needed. I'd been so excited to have Cardinal Woolsey's chosen for this television show. How had it all gone so terribly wrong? In one day?

Following his instructions, I phoned Charlie and asked if it would be all right for me to take the cast and crew over to Frogg's Books. "There's a problem with my shop."

"Bad luck." He was obviously surprised by my request but immediately said of course. I was welcome to it. And did I need him to come over?

It was his day off and the bookstore was closed, so I appreciated the offer. However, we kept keys to each other's shops, and so I told him I could manage.

"Lucy? Is everything all right?"

I didn't want to lie, so I asked him why he was asking. He seemed to think about it for a moment and then said, "I don't know. You sound odd."

"I'm fine. I've just got a little problem with my shop. I'll explain it all to you later."

Charlie was nothing if not a gentleman, and British, so as curious as he might've been, he wouldn't ask questions. In fact, he immediately apologized for seeming nosy. "Yes, of course. Sorry to press you. You'll tell me all in good time."

Once I had permission to use Charlie's shop, I phoned Molly, the show producer. Before I could say anything, she said, "Lucy, Lucy. Good. So glad I caught you. I've got an idea for some separate segments. Thought we might—"

Before she could go on, I interrupted. Once Molly got going, she might talk for half an hour. Also, I strongly suspected that she was trying to rearrange things to stop Enid from monopolizing the program again. Who could blame her? Oh my gosh, maybe Molly had murdered Enid. It was certainly an efficient way to stop the woman monopolizing Teddy's attention and ruining the program.

"Molly, I've got a problem with the shop. Can we meet at Frogg's Books? If we could put the students off for an hour, I'd like to see you by myself."

"Good heavens. What is it? Have you had a flood or something? Please tell me it wasn't a fire. We have some equipment still in your shop."

I almost smiled at how one-track her mind was. Almost.

"No. I don't want to talk about it on the phone. I'll explain when I see you. I just wanted to make sure I had your permission to phone all the students and put them off."

"Yes. If you must. I can get Becks to do it. And we'll sort out the crew to come later as well."

I didn't have the heart to tell her that I didn't think anyone was going to be doing any filming today. Better to tell her in person.

"Would you phone Teddy? If I do it, he'll chuck a wobbly. But if the news comes from you, he'll be polite."

"Fine."

Ian had overheard my side of the conversation, and when I was done, he said, "Good. I'd better get back downstairs." To my surprise, he reached out and touched my shoulder. "Are you going to be all right?"

I knew I'd be better once Enid Selfe, or what was left of her, was taken away. But I just nodded.

He left, and I curled up with Nyx.

When I phoned Teddy's hotel, Douglas picked up the phone. I explained my mission, and he said, "Fine. Have they fired that Enid woman?" From the sound of his voice, he'd heard all about how she derailed the filming the day before.

"I don't know."

"Well, you can tell Enid Selfe from me that today's class is being held in Prague. No, wait a minute, not Prague. I like Prague. I wouldn't inflict that dreadful woman on such a nice city. Pittsburgh. Tell her it's in Pittsburgh."

In spite of my awful morning, I had to laugh. "What do you have against Pittsburgh?"

"I was there once in winter. Pittsburgh ruined a perfectly good pair of Ferragamo leather boots. Sending it Enid would even the score."

"Duly noted."

Douglas promised to tell Teddy about the new arrangements. "But I have to tell you, he's not looking forward to today. It's like someone let all the helium out of the balloon."

I wanted to tell him that he didn't need to worry about Enid anymore. Of course I couldn't. I also wanted to tell him to stop talking before he said anything he was going to regret. Should I pass on his comments about Enid to Ian?

Whether it was the right thing to do or not, I knew I wouldn't. I liked Douglas, and I liked Teddy. If they had murdered Enid, the police were going to have to discover it themselves. I wasn't going to be a snitch.

Nyx was a great comfort as I sat there trying not to listen to the sounds coming from downstairs. She was a warm weight on my lap, anchoring me to what was good and warm and alive.

I was sitting there staring into space when my cell phone rang. It was Rafe. "Lucy. What's going on?"

"What do you mean?" Did the man spy on me? He didn't even live here.

"Sylvia called me. She said there are police in the shop."

Dread clutched my chest. "She didn't come up through the trapdoor in the back room, did she? Did the police spot her?"

He must've heard the panic in my voice. "Of course not. She and your grandmother were heading home. They'd been out visiting."

Thank goodness for that. There were plenty of other ways into the tunnels.

I told him swiftly what had happened. It was a relief to be able to actually tell someone and not have cryptic phone calls without revealing any information.

"What are you doing now?"

"I'm sitting here in my flat. Waiting for enough time to pass until I have to go across to Frogg's Books and meet Molly."

"You've got nearly an hour then. Meet me at the brasserie on High Street."

I knew the restaurant. They did wonderful breakfasts,

though I wouldn't be able to face food. At least I could get out of here and away from the sounds downstairs.

"I'll get a table in the back," he said. "I'll meet you there, or do you want me to pick you up?"

I was completely confused. "Are you in Oxford?" He lived about half an hour's drive outside the city.

"I am. I had business that kept me here last night." It was easy to forget that he was at his sharpest when I was sound asleep. I had no idea what kind of business he'd been doing, and I didn't want to know.

"And what are you going to do in a restaurant?"

There was a thread of humor in his voice as he said, "Feed you. You haven't eaten anything this morning, have you?"

How on earth could he know that? I'd drunk about two sips of my coffee and a cup of herbal tea.

"It's important that you eat. And I want you out of that police crime scene. At least for an hour."

Even the thought of a short break filled me with relief. "Yes," I said. "I'll meet you there."

Telling Nyx to stay put, I grabbed my bag and ran down the main staircase and let myself out the front door of the flat, which let out into a small back garden. My snazzy new red car was parked in the tiny parking spot, but there was no point driving the short distance to High Street, so I grabbed my bicycle out of the shed. It didn't take me more than five minutes to bike up to the brasserie. I locked my bike and walked in. The place was about half full.

Rafe was in the back at a table that was quite isolated. I was certain he'd chosen it deliberately. He had a cup of coffee in front of him, but I doubted he was drinking it. I walked over, and he rose as I approached, polite as always. I sat down, and he studied my face. "You look pale."

I raised my eyebrows. "Not as pale as you."

He was always slightly taken back when I made jokes, but a vampire in mid-summer looks pale indeed.

I was about to tell him that I couldn't manage any food when the waitress arrived. She put a plate of cold smoked salmon and scrambled eggs in front of Rafe, a full English breakfast in front of me, and a plate of toast between us.

Without even asking, she filled my cup with coffee.

Rafe had ordered for me. Typical high-handed behavior. I was going to push my plate away when the scent of the food hit me and I realized how hungry I was. Maybe just a piece of toast.

I reached for a slice of toast and nibbled on it.

"I want to tell you about an idea I've had," Rafe said.

How did he do this? I'd come here filled with horror and dread, thinking we'd go over all the details together, and suddenly he was making me wonder about this idea of his.

I didn't care if it was the worst idea in the world. Anything that kept my mind off the horror in my shop was a good thing. I asked, "What's your idea?"

"Dublin."

"Dublin?"

"Yes. I want to take you there."

I took a sip of coffee. "You want to take me to Dublin?"

"Yes."

"Why?"

"Have you been there?"

"No. Never."

"It's a beautiful city. I've got some work to do at Trinity University. It would do you good to get away for a few days. Violet can watch the shop, and you can get those college girls in to help her."

I had always wanted to go to Dublin. And he was right, it would be good to get away, but how could Violet or Scarlett or anyone work in a store where someone had been murdered?

As though he'd read my thoughts, he said, "I have to go in a couple of weeks. Plenty of time to decide if you want to come with me or not. There's a little shop for sale that I think would make a perfect wool and knitting shop."

My egg was perfectly cooked, the yolk slightly runny. I forked it up with bacon and beans. While my mouth was too full to speak, he continued, "It would be an excellent opportunity for your grandmother to get out of Oxford. Sylvia and I have talked about this a great deal."

When I'd swallowed, I said, "But I'm not ready to franchise."

"Sylvia would fund the entire enterprise. There'd be no cost to you. But we'd like you to take charge of the shop. Let your grandmother work in it part-time and hire some extra help."

I would miss having Gran so close to me, and Rafe knew that. Gently he said, "She finds it very hard, you know, not being able to be seen in Oxford. But she won't leave because of you."

And I didn't want her to leave. He continued, "We chose Dublin because it's so close. It's the only place she's been willing to consider."

"Close? You have to cross an ocean. Close would be, I don't know, London or Birmingham, somewhere I could drive in an hour."

"Lucy, there are several flights a day to Dublin. You can be there in a couple of hours."

"It's not the same though. You have to book flights ahead. I wouldn't be able drive down and have a visit whenever I felt like it. See her every day."

"No. You wouldn't."

He ate the smoked salmon sparingly, but I knew he wouldn't eat the eggs. I leaned over and helped myself to the scrambled eggs.

"London and Birmingham are out precisely because they

are too close. Agnes knew people in both places." He had a point.

"You don't think any of her customers would go to Dublin?"

He smiled at me ruefully. "If it were up to me, your grandmother would go to New Zealand or Canada, but she's refused. Dublin is as far as she's prepared to go."

"Well, I will go look at the shop. I won't promise anything more."

"That's a good start."

We chatted a little longer, and before I knew it, I'd finished my breakfast, drunk a cup of coffee and had a refill. I checked the time on my cell phone. "I've got to get going."

He nodded with satisfaction. "You look better. You've got some color back."

"You know, one of the most annoying things about you is that you're always right."

He shook his head. "Not always."

I got up to leave and realized we hadn't talked about the murder at all. I turned back. "Don't you want to grill me for details about the dead woman?"

"Later. I wanted to give you a break."

Annoying or not, he could be very thoughtful. And he was right. I did feel better for a meal.

CHAPTER 8

$\mathcal{I}$ cycled back to my shop feeling better for breakfast, fresh coffee, and a break from the grisly discovery. However, my break was over. I suspected it was going to be a very long day.

Rafe and I had very deliberately not talked about the murder, but he'd know soon enough. He'd told me he'd known Enid Selfe before she showed up in my life this weekend. I wondered if he knew much about her past, like any enemies she might have had.

I was also fairly certain that Rafe would start his own investigation, no doubt aided by Theodore, the undead private investigator who had been a policeman in life. No doubt they'd be aided by any of the bored vampires who were currently awake and looking for something to do. It might be boredom that drove them, but the vampires in Oxford had proven themselves to be excellent amateur detectives. Unfortunately, they got a lot of practice.

I had a talent for stumbling upon suspicious deaths without even trying. We all have our talents, but I'd have preferred to be good at something useful, like fashioning balloon animals.

As I cycled down Harrington Street, I was pleased to see that Ian had remembered to get all the police and emergency vehicles out of the area. I very much hoped they had already moved the body. I didn't want to share my quarters with the deceased Enid Selfe any longer than I had to.

If it weren't for the light on inside my shop, I could easily believe it was empty. I rode on past, not even turning my head for a peek, and parked my bike in front of Frogg's Books. I was a few minutes early, so I let myself in with the spare key, put on some lights, and headed for the cupboard where I knew Alice and Charlie kept the kettle and tea things. I suspected that Molly was going to need a nice strong cup of tea for shock when she heard the news.

One of Alice's ideas since she'd been working for Charlie had been to start a book club at the shop. Charlie had first turned up his nose at the idea, and then they'd argued about what kind of book club it should be—he wanted to challenge readers intellectually, and she wanted to choose books that were more accessible but still open to debate. Since she was the one who ran the book club, naturally, she managed to get her own way.

I set up the table and chairs that they used for book club in the back room, and then I waited. I wasn't terribly surprised when Molly didn't show up alone but had brought Becks along with her. She came in full of energy and the kind of focused determination that impressed me even when I wasn't suffering from shock. As it was, I felt numb and rather stupid, while they seemed keen and far too full of purpose. The first words Molly said were, "Your shop looks all right, Lucy. What's going on?"

"It can't be a power outage," Becks continued, "because we saw lights on."

"No signs of flood. No fire." They glanced at each other, and I could tell they'd run various scenarios back and forth as they'd driven in. Together they said, "Was it some kind of home invasion?"

"Or is part of the house falling in?" Molly asked, looking anxious. "That happened to an uncle of mine once, termites. The whole staircase collapsed one day when he came down it. He was lucky all he did was break a leg."

Before their guesswork reached aliens in spaceships, I spoke up. "Why don't you both come into the back room and sit down? I've made tea."

That's how English I'd become. Before even giving bad news, I felt they should have tea in front of them. It wasn't so much a barrier against bad news as a cure-all. Not that this could be cured, of course, but at least drinking tea gave them something to do while they absorbed the terrible news.

Molly appeared irritable. "We really don't have much time, Lucy. Forget the tea and tell us what's going on."

I would not be rushed. I took the fresh pot of tea, three cups, milk, sugar and the pocket of rich tea biscuits that I'd found in the cupboard into the back room. I'd already organized chairs and switched on lights. They could follow me or not.

Naturally, they did. Once we were sitting down and they both had tea and I'd poured myself a cup for good manners, I said, "I've got some terribly bad news."

There was a tiny pause, and then Molly asked, "Well? What is it?"

There was no easy way to say this. "I came down early this morning to check that everything was ready for the filming today," I began. They were both staring at me with that laser gaze. "I found Enid Selfe in my shop."

Molly's eyes flew open wide. "Does that woman have no sense of decorum? She showed up at your shop at the crack of dawn?"

I tried not to relive those terrible moments, but, of course, as I told the women, I saw it all again before me. "I don't think she did arrive at the crack of dawn. I think she might've been there all night."

"What? She slept over in your store?"

I wasn't doing this at all well. I shook my head. "I'm sorry to tell you this, but Enid was dead."

They exchanged glances and stared at me again in tandem. Molly looked like someone who's predicted disaster and been proven right. "Was it termites? Did a rotten beam fall on her or something?"

I almost wished I did have a shop full of termites so I wouldn't have to tell her the truth. "No. It wasn't termites."

Molly shook her head quite firmly. "No. She can't be dead. We're only one day into filming. Nobody dies until the show is wrapped." She didn't sound as though she were joking, more as though it was in the contract everyone signed. Show up on time, follow Teddy's instructions, oh, and don't drop dead.

Becks seemed slightly more human. "Lucy, how awful for you. You found her? Dead?"

"I did."

"I'm so sorry. Was it a heart attack, do you think?"

"Or a stroke?" Molly suggested. "Maybe an aneurism. She didn't look sick yesterday." Then she clutched her chest. "Tell me it wasn't anything infectious."

Here we went again with the guessing game. Where was Ian? He told me he'd be here. "The police are still determining the cause of death." I pushed the packet of cookies toward them. "Rich tea?"

Molly said, "It must have been a brain aneurysm."

Oh, I wished.

Ian arrived soon afterward. I told him in an undertone that I had already spilled the beans, as he was late and I couldn't hold them off. "I told them she was dead but not how."

He didn't seem too perturbed. "How did they take the news?"

"Like it was an inconvenience to filming."

"But they seemed surprised?"

"Yes."

"Still, they are in films. I suppose they could be acting."

I didn't bother telling him they were producers, not actors. He'd find out for himself soon enough.

Two uniformed officers came in behind Ian. He said, "As the knitting students arrive, keep them in the back room. We'll interview each of them separately. We can do one in the front room." He raised his eyes to the ceiling. "Is Charlie up there?"

"No. I think he's with Alice." Alice lived in a little house that was much nicer than Charlie's rather ramshackle flat above the shop. He seemed to spend a lot of his time there these days.

Ian said, "Good. You've got the keys for upstairs?"

I did. I hadn't checked with Charlie first, but I doubted he'd mind if his flat was used as an interview room to trap possible murderers. Would he? "Let me run up and make sure it's tidy." I'd also quickly phone Charlie and make sure he was okay with this plan.

Charlie's flat was like Charlie: disorganized, bookish, and rather charming. At least the dishes were done and there weren't clothes all over the place. He picked up the phone right away. "Lucy. Did you get in all right?"

"I did. Thank you. Look, Charlie, the reason I needed your shop is that one of the students in the televised knitting class was murdered last night in my shop." It was a relief to be able to tell him the truth.

"Good Lord. Was it Enid Selfe?"

My jaw literally dropped. "How did you know?" I didn't want to add Charlie Wright to the list of suspects.

"Because she was uniformly unpleasant, self-absorbed and irritating. I'm a peaceful man, and I felt like doing her in myself." I thought of Ian downstairs and decided not to encourage Charlie in that line of conversation. Hurriedly I told him that Ian wanted to use his flat as well as the shop to conduct interviews. He said it was fine and just to make sure to lock up after they all left. "After all, if one of them is a murderer, they might also be a thief."

CHAPTER 9

We didn't have long to wait before the first arrivals. Annabel and Ryan came in together, chatting and laughing. They looked as though they'd grown quite close in the short time they'd known each other.

They must have picked up on the dark atmosphere, for when they got to the back room, where Molly asked him to sit down, Ryan asked, "What's going on? Why all the long faces?"

They glanced at Ian and probably thought he had something to do with the production company, so they didn't pay much attention. Molly said, "Let's wait until everyone is here."

They exchanged glances and then both sat down and took out their lacework and began to knit. Naturally, I hadn't even thought to bring mine with me. The knitting shop owner was the one who forgot her knitting. Figured. Still, in fairness to me, I was also the only one who knew about the murder. Frankly, it would be a while before I looked at knitting needles as anything other than a murder weapon.

Vinod arrived next, and about five minutes later, Helen and Gunnar walked in together.

Teddy came in, and to my surprise, Douglas was with him.

When everyone was assembled around the table, they looked at Molly for explanation, and all she said was, "This is Detective Inspector Ian Chisholm of Oxford CID. He wants to talk to us all."

Gunnar glanced up sharply. "Police? What are the police doing here?"

Helen looked around the table with a puzzled expression. "Should we wait for Enid?"

"With a bit of luck, she's not coming," Ryan muttered.

I thought he'd regret those words very soon.

Ian spoke up then. "I'm sorry to tell you all that Enid Selfe was found dead this morning."

"Blimey," Ryan said.

"But why are the police here?" Annabel asked, looking around as a uniformed officer came in.

Ian replied, "Because she was murdered."

Ryan went pale. "Look, what I said a minute ago, obviously, I didn't mean..."

"How?" Vinod asked. "How did it happen?"

I didn't think he'd answer but then, looking slowly around the table, he said, "It appears she was stabbed. With steel knitting needles."

There was stunned silence. Then Helen said, jerkily, "Knitting is supposed to be relaxing. Calming. It is not, normally, a murderous occupation."

Ian resumed. "We'd like to interview each of you separately."

Gunnar spoke up now. "But we barely knew the woman." The stress seemed to have made his Norwegian accent more pronounced. "I only met her the day before yesterday. I barely spoke to her."

"Nevertheless, sir. We do need to ask you some questions."

He looked at Molly. "Must I? There was nothing about this in the contract I signed with your production company."

Molly looked surprised at his vehemence. I think we all were. She said, "I can call our company lawyer, if you'd like."

Perhaps Gunnar realized that not wanting to be interviewed by police and demanding lawyers made him look guilty, so he shook his head. "No. It's all right. I have nothing to hide."

"What about the crew?" Ryan asked. "Why aren't they here to be interviewed?"

"We'll be talking to each of them once we finish here," Ian said. "We'll get started right away then." He glanced around the table as though carefully choosing his first victim. Everyone dropped their gazes to the table as though they could avoid being chosen first. I might've done the same, except that I knew he wouldn't choose me, as I'd already been interviewed. At the murder scene, which I could've done without.

Ian had the most updated list from Molly. He glanced at it now. "Teddy Lamont? Let's begin with you."

"Me?" Teddy squeaked. "Can Douglas come with me?"

"No. But he can be interviewed at the same time. Douglas, you'll be interviewed by my colleague, Inspector Lee."

Ian led the way, Teddy following, and then Inspector Lee, and finally Douglas. As Douglas passed my chair, he leaned down and whispered into my ear, "You know I was joking about what I said earlier on the phone, right?"

"Yes," I whispered back. I hadn't passed on what he'd said, and I had no intention of doing so. We exchanged glances, and he seemed to understand that I wouldn't run to Ian to report what he'd said.

Once they'd gone, a horrible hush fell over the rest of us. I stood up looking for something to do. "Would anyone like some tea?"

"I'd like a martini," Annabel said. I understood how she felt.

Molly said, "Becks, why don't you go out and get some coffees and pastries or something. It's bad enough we have to sit here in this ghoulish way. At least we could have something to eat."

Becks seemed only too happy to leave, but she came back in a few moments looking frazzled. "There's a police officer at the back door. He says no one can leave without DI Chisholm's permission."

"But that's ridiculous—"

"They're just doing their job," I said. "I can phone Elderflower Café, next door to my shop. I'm sure they'll deliver whatever we want."

Molly nodded, still looking upset. "Nothing like this has ever happened to me before. I had a job offer, you know, on *Antiques Roadshow*. I should've taken it. Nobody ever gets murdered on *Antiques Roadshow*."

Helen said, "I wouldn't have thought knitting was a particularly murderous occupation." She seemed obsessed with this notion.

I barely suppressed a bitter laugh. She had no idea.

While Becks collected food orders, the knitters all took up their knitting. However, it all looked rather halfhearted. Finally, Ryan threw down his knitting. "I can't believe I said that about wishing she wouldn't show up today." He glanced up. "They won't hold that against me, will they?"

"Of course not," Annabel said, soothing.

"But what will they ask us? What do they want to know? None of us knew her." He glanced around. "Did we?"

"Of course not," Gunnar said. "I come from Norway. I live in London. Very far from this Toad in the Hole place where she lived."

I bit back a smile. I completely understood how complicated he found English place names. "I think it was Stow-on-the-Wold."

He shook his head. "Incomprehensible English naming."

Helen looked at him. "That depends quite a bit on

language, surely? Not everyone would find Preikestolen simple to say."

He looked at her blankly. It was Annabel who answered. "Oh, yes. Pulpit Rock. I hiked there once. Beautiful scenery."

Gunnar dropped his gaze back to his knitting. "I am no hiker."

There was a moment of silence. He seemed as though he didn't recognize the name of a famous hiking destination in his own rather small country. Helen looked as though she was going to say more but shook her head slightly and went back to her knitting. I'd found that when murder entered a room, everyone suddenly looked suspicious.

Making a food order gave us something to do. Since I knew the Watt sisters who ran Elderflower, I offered to phone them with our order. I asked them if they had someone who could bring it over, knowing I was asking a big favor. Mary Watt said, "We saw an ambulance and a police car outside Cardinal Woolsey's this morning. Is everything all right?"

Florence and Mary Watt were lovely women who'd been great friends of Gran and treated me like a favorite niece. "I'm fine," I assured her. "I'll explain it all later."

Becks pulled out her cell phone, her tablet computer, and notepad and paper. She glanced up at Molly. "Do you want me to run the numbers on how much it will cost if we have to cancel this show? And should I draft a message to the people at Larch Wools?"

Molly shook her head quite violently. "Don't do anything yet. I'll make some calls and see what I can do." She sighed. "See what I can do."

A worry frown marred her forehead as she took her phone and headed into the stockroom and toward the back entrance. No doubt a police officer would be able to overhear her conversations, but we wouldn't.

The knitters all kept working, and the rhythmic clicking

and clacking of needles should've been soothing, but right now, knitting needles and soothing did not correlate in my brain.

Someone who'd kill a person in that fashion would need physical strength and probably some background in medicine in order to get through the ribs and pierce the heart. I watched each of the knitters wielding those needles with such expertise.

Gunnar's big hands were surprisingly adept with needles and wool. He'd definitely have the strength necessary. Vinod was a radiologist. He wasn't as physically strong as Gunnar, but he must know the human body quite well. Ryan was probably strong enough. I doubted Annabel had done it; same with Becks, Molly and Teddy. Douglas, though, he was big, strong and very protective of Teddy.

I noticed that while four of the knitters were going along quite smoothly, Helen's knitting was jerky and uneven. When I looked more closely, I could see that her hands were shaking badly. She was a science teacher. I bet she knew her way around a ribcage.

A welcome interruption from my dark thoughts occurred when the police officer brought in a dark green plastic crate. In it was a large thermos jug of coffee and plastic-wrapped plates of assorted pastries, cakes and sandwiches.

I wasn't hungry after my breakfast, but we all helped ourselves to coffee and food. I took a piece of lemon cake for comfort. About ten minutes later, Teddy returned with Ian Chisholm behind him. We all looked up, but Teddy didn't look particularly distraught.

Before Ian could pick another person to be interviewed, Helen spoke up. "Do you think I could go next?" she asked in a jerky voice. "I have a nervous condition, you see. Stress isn't good for me. If I could be interviewed now, then perhaps I could go home. I didn't bring my pills with me. So stupid."

"Yes, of course," Ian said. "Should I bring in a doctor?" I

noticed he hadn't offered to send her home without being interviewed.

She shook her head. "No. I'll be fine."

"Very well." She got up, saying she was sorry to the table in general, though I didn't think anyone particularly minded not having to go next. She was barely out of the room when Ryan asked Teddy how it had gone. The knitting guru shrugged his shoulders. "It was kind of exciting, really. He asked me if I had any reason to want Enid Selfe dead." He threw his arms up in a dramatic gesture. "What was I supposed to say? My mother always told me never to lie to the police. Of course I told him it was the best news I'd heard since culottes went out of fashion. I'm surprised he didn't arrest me then and there."

Somehow this brought a sense of humor and balance back to us. And it was a welcome relief. Ryan leaned forward. "What did he ask you? What do they want to know?"

Teddy opened his eyes wide. "I think they want to know whether you killed that woman or not. And if you did, one of you, for goodness' sake, tell the man so we can get on with this. I have a televised class to teach. And you know what they say. The show must go on." He looked at the silver thermos jug. "Is that coffee?"

I was closest, so I poured him a cup.

Douglas returned then, so I poured him a coffee too. "Thanks. I need this," he said, helping himself to a Bakewell tart.

The officer invited Vinod to go next.

When they'd left, Molly said, "I'm so glad you're willing to go on with the show." She sounded dizzy with relief.

Around a large bite of his tart, Douglas said, "Teddy always fulfills his commitments."

"How can you think of your TV show when a woman's dead?" Annabel asked.

Teddy reached for a shortbread cookie. "Of course I'd love

to solve a murder. Who wouldn't? But that's the dishy inspector's job. Mine is to teach knitting. We're on a schedule, and I'd like to stay on it. Enid Selfe has caused us enough trouble. I don't want her derailing the rest of this project."

He sounded extremely selfish and cold-blooded, but I couldn't blame him. Douglas nodded in support.

Molly came around the table to where he was sitting. "Teddy. I'm so, so sorry."

"Well, I wouldn't wish anyone dead, but you must admit not having another day of filming with that woman will do us all a huge favor."

Molly looked delighted at his words. "You're really willing to continue?"

"Of course I am. I'm a professional. Besides, I'm launching a book, and this is all part of the promotion. It's a wonderful opportunity for both Larch Wools and Lamont Enterprises to gain market share. I don't see why that should change just because of a crime that I certainly didn't commit."

She let out a huge sigh. "That's wonderful news. I know we can edit around Enid without having to cut out too much. But all our advertising says six knitters. We need another one."

She looked to me. "Lucy, do you think you could find someone from your customers? Someone discreet who could slip into Enid's spot? If they look a little bit like her, then it will be an easier editing job."

Someone who wouldn't mind replacing a dead woman? Before I could say anything, Teddy wiped his mouth and announced, "I have the perfect person. You want another woman of a certain age, don't you? And I want someone who doesn't keep talking trash to me. What about that lovely lady I gave the proof of my book to, Lucy? What was her name?"

"Margot Dodeson?"

"Yes. The dear lady. She seemed grateful and very happy to

learn from me. I think she lives locally—well, she must, as she came to the book signing. What do you think?"

Molly squinted, concentrating. "You mean that mousy woman who was scared of her own shadow but followed you with worshipful eyes?"

He chuckled. "Yes. Exactly that one."

I couldn't think of anyone better than Margot Dodeson, and I said so. "You're exactly right. She's got similar coloring to Enid, is in the same age bracket, and she's local. The only problem will be getting her to agree. She's very shy, as you may have noticed."

Teddy sighed. "Believe me, after the ordeal of yesterday, shy is good. Shy is very good."

I glanced around the table and then to Molly. "But are you absolutely certain you're going to continue?"

"Absolutely." Then she smiled a very confident producer's smile at the assembled knitters. "As soon as we wrap this up, we'll get back to filming. I don't suppose we'll even go a minute beyond the time you've all agreed to in your contracts." Oh, that was smooth, the way she edged in that they'd all signed contracts.

There was some nervous shuffling, and Ryan looked as though he might say something, but it was Annabel who spoke up. "So long as I don't have to take more time off work, I'm in." It seemed that once she had spoken, everyone was in agreement. I supposed they all wanted to make sure they didn't do anything that made them look suspicious.

"Great. Great," Molly said. "And we'll wrap it all up next weekend. Lucy? Could you phone Margot?"

"And do I tell her why we're asking her to take over in Enid Selfe's place?" I did not relish this conversation.

"No. No. The police wouldn't want that. Just say that one of the knitters had to drop out suddenly. Tell her that Teddy asked for her specially."

He smiled at me. "It's true. I did ask for her specially. If you have any trouble convincing her, put me on the phone with her."

However, the extra influence wasn't necessary. Margot Dodeson seemed thrilled to be asked and, apart from saying she was sorry someone had to drop out, asked no difficult questions.

Like me, Teddy Lamont hadn't thought to bring his knitting with him. Perhaps he didn't even have a project on the go. Instead, he fiddled with his cell phone. Occasionally he would toss a nugget of information at Molly. "I've got an email from the head of Larch Wools. She's suggesting that if this goes really well, we might want to do something similar around my next book."

Molly stared at him. "If this goes really well?"

He nodded. "We'll get through this. And depending on how the show's received, I'd consider another one."

He was flipping from screen to screen and sending rapid-fire texts out with his thumbs like a teenager with ADD. Suddenly, he dropped the phone as though it were a live electric wire and he was standing in water. He went pale. "What the—"

CHAPTER 10

e all stopped what we were doing. Every knitter paused. Molly glanced up from her computer. "What is it?" Becks finally asked him.

He picked up his phone and pushed a lot of buttons. "Nothing. Sorry, I read that wrong. It was nothing. Nothing at all."

But it did not look like nothing at all. He sat there for a few more minutes, clearly agitated, and then he asked, "Has anyone told us when we can go? I've got things to do. I'm a busy man."

Molly had obviously had a lot of experience soothing frazzled celebrities. She said, "I'm sure they'll let us go as soon as they can. When that detective comes back, I'll ask him."

Teddy nodded. And he said, "Douglas, I need to talk to you privately."

He glanced toward the back door. "Are the cops still guarding the back door? Why are they treating us like criminals? It's ridiculous. I teach knitting. I don't go around murdering people."

I tried to think of somewhere private, but there were interviews going on in the bookstore and in Charlie's flat upstairs. The stock room contained the back door where an officer was stationed. Teddy was right. They were treating us, if not like criminals, at least with suspicion.

Douglas looked concerned by Teddy's agitation. He turned to Molly. "Is there somewhere in this godforsaken bookshop that we could have some privacy?"

This was obviously a very new situation to her, as it was to all of us. She said, "I'll talk to the police officer at the back door. I'm sure he'll let you stand a little way away, out of earshot. That's probably the best I can do for privacy."

He didn't look happy, but he agreed. The three went out. I'd never seen Teddy look so serious. That sprightly energetic man seemed subdued, and when he walked out of the room, it was as though his shoes were made of cement.

When they were gone, we all looked at one another.

"What was that about?" Ryan asked Annabel.

She shook her head. "I don't know, but Teddy Lamont looked frightened."

Molly came back and sat down again, but she kept looking toward the back as though hoping Teddy would return.

Douglas and Teddy weren't gone for long. When they came back, Teddy did not look relieved. If anything, he looked more troubled. Douglas had a very determined expression on his face.

"We should never have agreed to do this lace teaching. I had a feeling. I had a bad feeling, Douglas."

The big man put his hand on Teddy's shoulder. "You didn't do anything wrong. But you have to tell them."

"Tell us what?"

Ian walked in, Helen trailing behind. She reminded me of someone coming out of hospital after a major operation. She looked weak, pale and shaky. Teddy didn't look thrilled the detective had overheard him and Douglas.

There was utter silence for a moment, and then Douglas said, "Go on. It'll be okay."

"Easy for you to say. The murderer didn't use your phone."

That got all of our attention. Vinod and his detective came in behind Helen, and Vinod said, "I beg your pardon?"

Ian asked, "Did I hear you correctly?"

Teddy obviously enjoyed being the center of attention, but I thought in this instance, he'd have been happier without the audience. His tone was curt. "Yes, you did. I wouldn't make that up. The murderer used my phone."

He flicked back to his texts, and I could see that his hands were unsteady. He read aloud. "This is Teddy. Meet me at Cardinal Woolsey's at midnight. The door will be unlocked. I want to speak with you privately." He glanced up. "First, I would never have sent that woman a text. Second, she is the last person I would want to meet in the middle of the night."

He glared at Ian as though he might get an argument. "And who announces themselves? This is Teddy?" He shook his head. "I did not send that text."

Ian nodded but only said, "We'll have to take that into evidence, sir." It was pretty obvious to all of us that there wouldn't be any forensics evidence left. If there'd been any fingerprints left on the phone, Teddy had wiped them away long ago with his restless fingers. He handed it over reluctantly. "Okay, but that's my lifeline. I'll need it back as soon as possible."

"We'll do everything we can, sir." Then, somewhat surprisingly, Ian pulled up a chair and sat around the table with the rest of us. Ryan and Annabel, who'd been waiting to be led away, glanced at each other. To Teddy, he asked, "Did you leave your phone anywhere yesterday? Did you lend it to anyone?"

"No, I didn't lend my phone to anyone. I told you, it's my lifeline. It goes with me everywhere."

"Did you ever let it out of your sight?"

Teddy was less sure about this one. Helen said, "We were all told we couldn't have our personal belongings visible, and Molly stressed that we had to turn phones off."

Teddy nodded. "That's right. She read the riot act to me, too."

Helen continued, "I remember seeing your phone in your jacket pocket." It was true. Teddy had been wearing an oatmeal linen jacket when he'd arrived. He'd taken it off and tied the sweater around his neck as though putting on a costume.

The producer had made us put our coats and bags in the back room with the extra furniture. Molly explained all this to Ian, who asked, "So anyone who was in the shop yesterday could've gone into the back and used Teddy's phone?"

Teddy shrugged. "I suppose so."

Vinod stared at him. "Isn't your phone password-protected?"

Douglas shook his head, looking disgusted. "How many times have I told you to make your password less obvious?"

Teddy immediately went as sulky as a toddler who's been told off. "It's not that easy to figure out. It's easy for you because you already know it."

Douglas looked around at us and opened his arms. "Any guesses?"

Teddy was a nice guy but pretty full of himself. And he'd want something easy to remember. I said, "TEDD?" My second guess would be TEDL.

Teddy looked horrified. "Lucy, was it you?"

"Of course it wasn't me." And now I wished I hadn't been so quick to guess his password. I looked around at the table. "Who else guessed TEDD?"

Helen put up her hand. Vinod put up his hand.

Gunnar shook his head. "I did not guess."

Annabel said, "My first guess was LACE, but if that wasn't right, I'd have tried TEDD."

Ryan said, "I figured it was TEDD."

"Okay." Teddy threw up his hands. "Okay. As soon as I get that phone back, I'm changing the password." And then the pout slid back down over his face. "And Douglas, you'll have to remember it for me."

No doubt his next password would be something like DOUG.

Ian looked like a detective who had detected that his main suspects were a bunch of idiots. He stared down at the phone as though it might speak to him. The case was a Teddy Lamont design. How easy it would be to spot which smartphone was his. "Right. We know the killer sent a text from Teddy's phone. That's progress." He looked around the table. "That means it could've been any one of you, and, Molly, I'll need a list of every person on the crew who came in that day. Not just the ones working there. Did anyone come in to bring extra equipment, bottled water, anything?"

She nodded. "Becks and I will get right on it."

He turned to me. "Apart from cast and crew, did anyone else come into your shop yesterday?"

I shook my head. "I don't think so."

Even the vampires had stayed away.

It was no fun thinking that I might be sitting at a table with a murderer. No doubt everyone else who wasn't the killer was having the same thought.

"Wait," Ryan said. "You took your phone when you went out to get coffee, right?" Immediately, I recalled how frustrated Teddy had been with Enid and how he'd snapped that he needed a coffee break.

"Yes," Teddy said.

"Where did you go?" Ian asked. "And what time was this?"

"I told you when you interviewed me. I left the class about eleven. I was back about half an hour later."

Ian looked around. "Is that correct?" Before Teddy could protest, he said soothingly, "It's easy to mistake time."

We all looked at one another. Molly said, "That sounds right. I can check with the techs to be certain."

Ian nodded. "And when you left the class, you took your phone with you."

"Obviously."

"Right. Annabel and Ryan, we'll interview you now. The rest of you are free to go."

It was such a shock to be allowed to leave that we all sat there for a minute as though waiting for him to change his mind.

He didn't, and so everyone left but me. I had to stay behind and lock up. I didn't really mind, as I wasn't thrilled at the idea of going back to the scene of the crime, which also happened to be my business and home.

Since I was all alone without even my knitting, I perused the books. The ones back here were mostly older titles. All the good stuff was out front. I could hear the rumble of conversation. Two male voices, so Ian must be talking to Ryan. Annabel would be upstairs.

I found a book about Roman Britain and settled to read while I waited.

The Romans were beginning to lay the Fosse Way, a road that crossed much of England in a straight line, when Ian and Ryan came into the back room. Told he could leave, Ryan said, "Tell Annabel I'll see her back at the hotel."

When he was gone, Ian seemed to hesitate, then said, "Lucy, the attack on Enid Selfe was brutal. You saw the corpse. And whoever killed her managed to get into your shop."

He wasn't telling me anything I didn't know, but still, I shivered.

"I don't think it's wise for you to stay there alone. Not until we have whoever did this in custody."

Of course, he didn't know that the vampires would be vigilant if they thought I was in trouble. I knew them. They'd keep watch over me and make sure I was safe. "Do you really think I'm in danger?"

"Until we know who did this and why, it's impossible to say. The attack took place in your shop. Knitting needles were used. It could be directed at you."

Again, nothing I hadn't already thought about, but I didn't want to dwell on it.

"I can send a patrol around, but we don't have the resources to station an officer in your home."

And that was the last thing I'd want. Not with my undead neighbors walking around all night. "No. It's fine. I'll be fine."

"Is there someone you can stay with for a few days?"

"Yes." I could stay with Violet, though I hated being driven from my home.

"Good."

Annabel and Inspector Lee arrived then, and I ushered everyone out before making sure Charlie's home and shop were locked up safely.

I'd gathered up the coffee things and packed them back into the crate. As I walked out into the afternoon sunshine, I thought I'd take a drive in my new car, go shopping, anything to stay away from my own home.

The crime scene.

CHAPTER 11

*W*hen I got to Elderflower Tea Shop, I could tell that the Miss Watts had been watching for me. Both of them met me at the door. It was fairly busy with afternoon tea customers, but the owners gave me all their attention. "Come and sit down, Lucy," Florence said, taking the crate from my hands and putting it down in a corner. A busboy spotted it and immediately came to whisk the crate away. Cool. They had hired efficient staff this summer.

"Come and have a cup of tea and tell us all about it."

They took me to a quiet table far from the popular window tables so we wouldn't be overheard. "We were so worried that something might have happened to you. Agnes would never forgive us. Ever since she passed, we've felt responsible for you, dear."

I shook my head, feeling warm inside that they cared. "I'm fine, but someone died in Cardinal Woolsey's."

Mary put a hand to her chest. "Oh, no. Some of your customers are quite old."

"But there was so much police activity," Florence continued.

These two might be old, but they were sharp. "I'm sorry to say someone was murdered in my shop last night."

"Oh, no. And when you've got that filming going on," Florence said.

I turned down the offer of cakes and sandwiches, but I accepted the offer of tea. We sat over a big pot, the three of us, while I told them what little I knew. I trusted these women, and so I shared the grisly discovery I'd found this morning.

"You must come and stay with us," Florence said firmly.

"I appreciate the offer so much, but I've already asked my cousin Violet." I hadn't yet, but I thought I'd be more comfortable staying with someone who knew about my secret gift.

"The nice girl with the odd hair who helps in your shop?"

"That's her."

"All right, dear, but you know you're always welcome. We've got the guest room all ready for you."

I thanked them again. I even accepted more tea, as I was in no hurry to get back to the shop. "Did you happen to see whether, um..."

"The body was taken away more than an hour ago," Florence said, correctly guessing my unspoken question.

"Oh, good."

"I believe there are still forensics people there, but most of the activity is finished," Mary continued. I imagined they'd been busy peeking out their windows all day in between serving customers.

As I got up to leave, Mary said, "Oh, Rafe was here earlier. He said he'd meet you at your place. Give him a ring."

"Thanks." I was relieved not to go home alone. I expect he'd known I would be.

I texted to let him know I was on my way, and when I walked around back to the lane where the entrance to the flat was located, I saw a familiar black Tesla. I was too glad to see him to accuse him of hovering.

He waited until we were upstairs to ask, "How are you holding up?"

His eyes scanned my face as though it would tell him more than my words would. "I'm fine. I'm guessing that between Sylvia, Gran and your contacts in the police, you know more than I do."

"Probably. I wasn't there, though. It must have been unpleasant."

A spurt of laughter was surprised out of me. "Unpleasant? Oh, yeah."

We sat in the living room. It was warm but not too hot, as I'd left the windows open. "Initial results are in from the coroner."

"Already?" That seemed really quick to me. "They couldn't have done an autopsy so quickly."

"No. But there's something I think you'll find very interesting."

I knew him. When he said interesting, he usually meant jaw-dropping. So I prepared myself. "What is it?"

"Your knitting friend, Enid Selfe—"

"She was no friend of mine."

He smiled slightly. "Enid Selfe, your murder victim—"

"Much better."

"Sylvia and I speculated, as I'm sure you did, that whoever killed her needed brute strength and a knowledge of human anatomy to get through the ribs and pierce the heart."

I shuddered, but he was right. I had thought those things. He said, "They were the right questions to ask. But it turns out she was already dead, or as good as dead, when those needles were plunged into her chest."

My eyes opened wide as I tried to take in this latest revelation. "She was already dead?" I could picture her in my mind as I'd found her that morning. "You mean somebody murdered her and then shoved knitting needles into her chest?"

"Yes."

"That was seriously ragey."

"Do you have any theories?"

"Me?"

"Well, she was killed in your store with your antique knitting needles. Doesn't the killing seem like it's directed your way?"

No. I did not want to think that. "First of all, they weren't my knitting needles. They were Gran's."

"Most of the world believes your grandmother is dead, which suggests they were directed your way."

"You're saying somebody wasn't happy with the customer service at Cardinal Woolsey's? So instead of writing a negative online review like anyone else in the world, they felt they had to go the extra distance?" My voice went shrill. I was not liking this theory.

"There are disturbed people in this world, Lucy. Have you had any angry customers? Somebody who seemed off?"

"Apart from Hester, you mean? She's the angriest person I know. She was definitely not happy that she couldn't be part of the television show." But Hester as a knitting-needle-stabbing killer? I thought Hester would kill the normal vampire way. Unless she was trying to send suspicion elsewhere. "Did you increase her allowance like she wanted you to?"

"No," Rafe said. "You think she's getting back at me through you?" We both thought about that for a minute. "It's cool and calculated. I wouldn't have thought Hester was intelligent enough."

I'd been joking. "You don't really think Hester did this, do you?"

"Someone or something did this. Until we have more information, we need to be open to all possibilities."

"So how exactly was Enid Selfe killed?" I hoped it was less horrific than what had been done postmortem.

"She'd sustained a blow to the back of her skull. That's what killed her. She probably never knew what hit her."

That was good to hear. "Any idea on the murder weapon?"

"No. That's where we'll have to wait for the full report. Could be a rock, a candlestick, steel rod, something that would do a lot of damage, and yet, that somebody could carry without arousing suspicion."

"Carrying a rock or a fire poker down Harrington Street would look strange."

"Point taken. However, we have to remember that this happened late at night. It's quiet here then." He paused. "For mortals."

I'd forgotten to tell him about Teddy's text message, so I did.

"So the killer lured Enid Selfe here to the shop at midnight. Presumably she was killed right away."

"But Rafe, midnight isn't very late. I'm sometimes still up then." Nyx came in the window then, jumped down and walked straight over to jump on Rafe's lap ignoring me completely. Never mind that I was the one who fed her, kept her in water and cat treats, and oh, yeah, she was my familiar. "I did hear noises downstairs. I just thought it was one of the vampires who'd come up to collect knitting supplies." It happened often enough that I'd learned to tune out any peculiar noises coming from my shop in the middle of the night.

"What time, exactly, did you hear those noises?"

I looked at the clock. "I honestly don't know. Maybe twelve-thirty?"

"I suspect you heard the murder."

I closed my eyes against the knowledge that maybe I could have saved Enid if I'd climbed out of bed and investigated those noises.

Rafe knew me so well. "Lucy, if you'd gone down there, there might be two victims instead of one."

He was right, of course, but it still didn't make me feel any better to know a woman had been killed in my store, close enough that I could hear it, and I'd done nothing to prevent her murder.

"The fact that the killer chose midnight suggests that person didn't know you very well and didn't realize you live above the shop. That helps narrow down the suspects."

I couldn't do anything to help Enid, but I would do my best to solve her murder. From the look on Rafe's face, he was just as determined to help me. Rafe could be high-handed and controlling, but he was also someone who had my back. If anyone did anything that hurt me, he wouldn't rest until justice was done. I also knew that he was modern enough and perhaps civilized enough that his way of administering justice wouldn't involve a lifeless body sucked of all its blood. At least, I hoped not. For while he was tame and civilized, there was always a hint of the animal. I wished it didn't attract me so much, but it did.

I thought of that woman lying there in my shop, dead. "Rafe, you've been around a long time. Why do people kill each other?"

He took my question seriously, which was one of the nicest things about Rafe. He always took my questions seriously. "I have been around a long time. I don't suppose there's much I haven't seen. Men kill in wartime, obviously. When I was a young man, it was fashionable to fight for honor, though that seems to have gone out of fashion."

I was obviously not getting what I wanted, so he paused to think. Then he began to enumerate on the long, white fingers of one hand. "A person kills to protect those he loves. To guard a secret. For revenge. To right a wrong. To stop the victim from doing something or telling something." He looked uncomfortable and wouldn't meet my eye. "Some people kill for sport or to assuage boredom. And others kill for the pleasure of it."

I swallowed hard. "Pleasure?"

"It's a twisted sickness, taking pleasure in having the ultimate power over another, that of life and death."

"Do you think that's why Enid Selfe was killed?" Why would I grab onto that motive of all others? Maybe because it sounded random, like a crazed maniac had got hold of her, so her death was completely unrelated to Cardinal Woolsey's or the televised knitting lessons. But I'd barely got the question out, hopefully, when Rafe shook his head.

"I suspect this latest murder victim was killed for one of the classic reasons."

"Is being really annoying one of the classics? I admit to being tempted to violence myself."

"Tempted and acting are worlds apart, Lucy. Whoever took that woman's life was more than irked. The violence of the act suggests pent-up anger left to fester, perhaps for years."

"Years?" This was almost as good as the crazed random maniac theory. "You mean whoever killed her wasn't related to the TV show or my shop in any way?"

"Possibly."

"I've never thought of knitting as a vicious activity before."

"It isn't," Rafe said, lifting Nyx off his lap. He stood up and began to pace. "No, I don't think the viciousness was directed at the hobby of knitting itself. It was directed at you, here, at this shop, or at Enid Selfe and her connection with this shop."

"But we've already been through all that. If it wasn't Hester, and I don't think it was, then who would be that angry?"

"You've done something that's brought out some deep-seated rage in somebody. Possibly someone rather unstable."

"But what? The only thing remotely different is—" I think it hit us at the same time, and we stared at each other. At the very same moment, we said, "The television show."

Could that be it? Could someone be so enraged with the production company or Teddy Lamont or somebody associated with Larch Wools that they would want to destroy one of the knitters? It seemed a little far-fetched, but so was finding a middle-aged woman with knitting needles sticking out of her chest. And yet, it had happened. To me.

"Okay, so, if someone wanted to hurt the production company, maybe stop filming, I can see why they would kill someone in my shop. It's definitely interrupted the filming. But why Enid? Why not kill the producer or a cameraman?" I gulped. "Or Teddy?"

He shook his head. "I don't know."

"The killer knew Enid would come to Cardinal Woolsey's late at night if Teddy asked her. I think we have to start there. Whoever killed her was someone she knew."

"It could've been someone she'd met at the book signing. She was certainly making the rounds." And he would know, since she'd been hitting on him.

"If someone wanted to derail the TV show they should have left Enid Selfe alive. She was making Teddy crazy with her questions and criticism."

Rafe paused to look at me. "Do you think Teddy Lamont did this?"

"No. But I can't think of anyone who would've done this. Teddy certainly had a motive in that she was ruining the show and doing her best to make him look like a shoddy knitter and a bad teacher."

"Do we know where Teddy was last night? Does he have an alibi?"

"Rafe, it was after midnight. Everyone except you and my other undead friends is usually asleep at that time. No one can have a decent alibi. They'll all say they were sleeping in bed, and for most of them, that will be true."

"That's a good point. Well, wouldn't Douglas have noticed if Teddy wasn't there?"

"He could be a deep sleeper. He might not have noticed. Or he could be in on it. Maybe one of them lured the woman here and distracted her while the other one clubbed her over the head." In fact, if Teddy had anything to do with it, I was pretty sure that would've been how it went down. Teddy didn't look like the murdering type to me, but Douglas? I thought that Douglas was to Teddy the way Rafe was to me. He could be civilized and mild-mannered, but anybody who hurt the person he loved was going to pay. Douglas, I suspected, could be ruthless.

Rafe seemed to ponder this theory for a minute and then asked, "But how would they have gotten in?"

Oh, he was not going to like what I had to tell him next. I cringed as I said, "I gave Teddy a key."

I didn't have to wait long for his blast of angry words. "You gave a virtual stranger a key to your shop? Which connects to your home?" His voice rose a little, and it continued to rise as he finished his thought. "Where you live alone?" By the time he got to *alone,* the word seemed to echo around the flat like a squash ball bouncing off the walls of an enclosed court.

"He's not a stranger. I carry his magazines. I've seen him on YouTube. He's nice."

Rafe let out a slow breath. "You'd better tell me who else had keys."

"Molly. Becks. The cameraman because he had to set up early. Molly assured me they are all bonded, and she personally vouched for them."

When he raised his brows, I said, "Molly is the producer, and Becks—her real name is Rebecca—is her assistant. It just made sense since they were going to be in and out of here all the time. I think Molly might've had a key cut for the lighting and props guys." At his horrified expression, I said, "I'm not here all the time. It was much easier since they were coming at the crack of dawn and leaving whenever they felt like it just to give them a key rather than me having to keep running downstairs to let them in."

"Anybody else?"

I tried to think. "No, I think that's it."

"You didn't give out keys to all the participants in the knitting show? I'm sure they all seemed nice."

"Okay, you don't have to be sarcastic. I did not give out keys to the participants because I knew I'd be there at the same time so I could let them in."

He shook his head. "Still, how hard would it be for somebody to pocket one of those keys and have another one made? There are so many floating around, you'd never know."

I felt kind of grumpy. "You should put Alice and Charlie on the list too. We have each other's keys in case one of us needs to use the other's space. Which turned out to be a good thing today, when I had to move the whole enterprise over to Frogg's." The Miss Watts next door also had my key, but if Rafe didn't remember that, I wasn't going to tell him. Harrington Street was a friendly place, and most of the retailers had been here a long time. We knew each other; we trusted each other. I didn't want to start being the kind of person who thought one of the most popular knitting gurus in the world might be a murderer. At least, not until it was proven.

I could tell Rafe was holding himself back from blasting me for my over-trusting nature, but it was an effort. He paced a bit quicker and, when he had himself under control, asked me for the printout of all the students, and he asked for a crew list as well. I printed out two fresh copies, one for each of us.

He said, "Theodore could be a big help here. Maybe he can check into the backgrounds of some of the people on these lists. I'll focus on Teddy and Douglas, since you can't seem to accept the possibility that they could be brutal murderers."

"And me?" I asked him sweetly. "What am I allowed to use my pretty little head for?"

"You will keep your eyes and ears open. And, as much as

you can in casual conversation, find out more about each of the people in the class."

I nodded. "So we're looking at two possibilities then. One, that some person or persons had it in for the production company, Teddy Lamont or Cardinal Woolsey's. And two, that person or persons had a real hate on specifically for Enid Selfe."

He said, "Except, of course, there's the possibility that both are true. Somebody wanted to stop the production or cause either Teddy or Cardinal Woolsey's trouble, and perhaps they chose Enid Selfe because they also had it in for Enid.

"And Lucy," he said, his pale eyes boring into mine, "do not forget that whoever did that terrible thing is capable of killing again."

"I know. I will keep my eyes and ears open, and if I hear anything else downstairs, I'll call the police."

He made a sound that I swear was more of the growl of a wild animal than a human sound. "You won't be anywhere near the shop until this murder's solved. You're coming home with me."

Seriously, I did appreciate that Rafe hadn't got used to the fact that men couldn't treat women the way they did when he originally came into manhood during Queen Elizabeth's time. And I mean the first Queen Elizabeth. But he could still shock me with his high-handedness.

I put my hands on my hips and stared up at him. It's always hard to stare down someone who is taller than you are. "I am not going to your house. I can go to Violet's place."

"Violet is a silly witch who can't even control a love potion. She lives alone and has no self-defense skills or military training. She can't keep you safe."

"Well, that's where I'm going." Probably.

"Lucy, you can come to my home willingly, or I can throw you over my shoulder and carry you. The choice is yours."

CHAPTER 12

I decided to ignore his barbarian suggestion and bent my attention, instead, to the list of knitting student bios. "I hate to think one of them did it." I'd come to like this odd collection of knitters.

Rafe said, "You've now spent a full day of knitting with these people and the better part of a very stressful day, when they were all interviewed by police and treated like murder suspects. People reveal a lot about themselves when they are under stress. And you're very observant. What did you notice?"

It was nice of him to say that I was observant, but I was also under stress. Sure, it was bad to be interviewed by the police about a murder, but it was a hair more stressful when you were the one who found the dead person. However, I knew he was right, and I tried to focus.

Since we were both looking at the paper, we naturally went in the order that the students were listed. Enid was the first one. Even looking at her picture, grainy as it was from my photo-copier, I felt the awful sadness that her life had been cut off so abruptly. She'd had plans. She'd wanted to get married again. She was knitting lace for her daughter to wear at Oxford.

She hadn't even enjoyed her last day on earth. She'd been so filled with irritation at Teddy that his knitting didn't come up to her standards that I felt even worse for her.

"Enid Selfe. I only know what's in this bio and what she told us during class. She lived in Stow-on-the-Wold. Her bio says she's a homemaker. I know she was married three times and on the lookout for number four." I thought of the way she'd been batting her eyes at Rafe and resting her well-manicured hand on the chest that held his cold heart. "You probably know more about her than I do."

I could see him focusing on her photograph, almost as though trying to bring her face into focus. "I've met so many people in the course of my existence. I simply cannot keep track of them all. She reminded me that we'd met at an event for Friends of the Bodleian."

While I understood that he had a point about the number of people he'd met in his long existence, it hadn't been that long ago. "Enid Selfe was the one hitting on you at the book signing. You must've smelled her with your sensitive nose because she'd doused herself with perfume and freshened up her makeup before wandering over to talk to you."

His nostrils quivered. "I do remember that smell. Why do women insist on drenching themselves with scent? Back in my day, there was logic behind the practice. We used perfumes to cover up the smells of the sewers and the odor of unwashed humanity. But today, people shower every five minutes. The last thing they need is to add artificial scent."

"I never wear perfume."

He looked at me in a rather disturbing way that made me wish I'd kept my mouth shut. "I had noticed."

His nostrils quivered again, and I knew that even now he could smell me. Awareness quivered down my spine and made me hold my gaze firmly to the papers in front of me. "You said she was a Friend of the Bodleian?"

"She was. One of her former husbands was something to do with the government. He had an interest in old manuscripts. She used to come with him. But then I didn't see them anymore. There was some sort of scandal, I believe."

At the word scandal, my ears perked up. "Scandal? What sort of scandal? The kind that leads to murder?"

"Some sordid affair. He ran off with someone else, I think." He looked up at my ceiling and half-closed his eyes. "No. She was the one who ran off with someone else. That's right."

Well, she'd certainly wanted to run off with Rafe the other night. "Do you think she ran off with someone she met at the book launch?" I shook my head. "Knowing Enid, she'd have wanted to see bank balances first."

He looked at me. "You really didn't like that woman, did you?"

"No one liked that woman. But I'm not just being catty." I looked over at Nyx. "No offense, Nyx. But I think she really did collect rich men. Or maybe all men. I don't know."

What else did I know about Enid? I thought back to the general conversation we'd exchanged over our knitting. It wasn't very consequential, not the kind of thing I really paid that much attention to. If I'd known she was going to be murdered, I'd have listened more closely. "I got the impression that money and status are very important to her. She dropped the name of the designer who decorated their home in Stow-on-the-Wold. Teddy knew the guy and looked impressed."

"How bourgeois."

"I know her daughters went to some fancy, expensive school. She made a big deal about how she had to throw her weight around at that school and make sure the girls got the proper instruction, and she was determined that they go to one of the top universities."

"And did they?"

"I don't think they've finished whatever you call high school over here. But she was convinced the eldest was coming here, to Oxford."

"What subject will she read?"

"I don't think Enid cared what they studied so long as they went to the right schools so she could drop into conversation, 'My daughter was at Oxford' or 'Of course my youngest is at Cambridge.'"

"So she's a snob. Not something that usually gets one killed. At least not in this country."

"I got the feeling that the only thing she cared about, apart from herself, was her daughters. She mentioned having to separate the older from an undesirable relationship."

"No doubt the girl was flirting with the dancing master or the under-gardener."

I couldn't help but chuckle. "If this were the 1800s."

"Well, whatever today's version is." He looked incredibly wise. "People don't change very much, you know."

I sighed. "Probably just someone who wasn't rich or titled at least."

Rafe glanced at his watch. "You should pack a bag. We need to get on our way."

Were we back to this? "Rafe, I am not sleeping at your house tonight."

"Nonsense. Of course you are. I've asked William to prepare dinner out on the terrace. He's gone to a lot of trouble for you, Lucy. And he gets very cross if he has to hold a meal."

I wanted to stamp my feet in frustration. He'd really taken advantage of me this time. He knew I liked William and I really liked his cooking. But I could play hardball too. "Fine. I'll come and eat William's no doubt delicious dinner, but I'm taking my own car, and I'm coming back here afterward."

He strode forward to me in two strides and grasped my shoulders. "Lucy. You know that if you return here, I will spend the entire night prowling around. With the heightened police security and nervous residents of Harrington Street, I'll attract attention. Is that what you want?"

He did not play fair. "You just said there will be heightened police security. You don't need to prowl around."

His eyes were steady on my face and oh-so-serious. "May I remind you that there is a deranged murderer on the loose and about thirty-five keys to your shop door floating around? Do you really think that anything would keep me away?" He held my shoulders even tighter. "I have to protect you. I must."

I suppose it was that almost desperate-sounding appeal in his voice. As though there had been women in the past that he hadn't been able to save. It annoyed me to give in, but I did at last. "Fine," I said, letting him know how cross I was. "But I'm only staying tonight."

Instead of arguing with me further, he simply said, "Thank you," and I felt how much he cared. I knew it was concern and affection driving him, but we were going to talk about this controlling behavior very soon.

Nyx yawned and stretched. I said, "Is she invited too?"

"You don't even have to ask."

It didn't take me long to pack. I pulled out an overnight bag and threw in a couple of summer dresses, two cardigans, some loungewear and underwear. I kept a toiletry bag in my bathroom for the odd time when I traveled. "Do you have a hair dryer?" I yelled from the bathroom.

"Of course," he said, sounding offended that I would even ask. I rolled my eyes at myself in the mirror in the bathroom. No doubt this was going to be like staying in a seven-star hotel, which perversely annoyed me even more. If I was sleeping on the couch so he could look after me, that would be one thing, but to stay in an elegant manor house, no doubt in a luxurious guest bedroom, seemed less like escaping danger than a retreat at the spa. Not that I had any objection to a retreat at the spa. I just didn't want Rafe to be providing it.

I liked to choose my own spas.

I didn't really like driving, even though I did have the beautiful new car that Rafe and the other vampires had given me for my twenty-sixth birthday, so it wasn't very difficult for Rafe to persuade me that I should drive with him. He said we could continue talking about all the other students while we were driving. Also, he claimed that he had business in Oxford the next morning so was going to be driving back anyway. It might even have been true.

Once we were purring along in the black Tesla, he said, "Ryan's next, I think."

I looked at the bios, though I had to maneuver around my cat. Nyx wasn't the type to travel in a crate. She was sitting on my lap. Her tail twitched back and forth so I felt as though I were being dusted.

"That's right. Ryan is in his thirties. His grandmother taught him to knit. I think he said she's Jamaican. Which gives him a connection with Annabel, who's also Jamaican."

Rafe glanced over at me. "Ryan's Jamaican? He looked Caucasian to me."

"Right. You're right. He was adopted by a mixed-race couple. I think he said his mother's Jamaican and his father's Irish." I nearly jumped up and down on the seat. "Oh, oh, and when we were talking, Enid asked him when his birthday was. It turned out she gave up a baby for adoption who would have been about the same age as Ryan."

"And does Ryan know his biological mother?"

I looked at his classically chiseled profile. "No. When Annabel joked that Enid could be his mother, he said if she was, he'd have to kill himself. Or her."

Rafe glanced over at me and then turned his gaze back to the road ahead. "Do you think she was Ryan's birth mother?"

"Isn't it possible? Maybe he'd always wondered, made up stories about the woman who really wanted him but had to give him up, and then he found out the true story and snapped. Maybe he killed Enid."

"We'll get Theodore to do some digging. If Ryan is her child, he had a very personal motive for killing her." He swerved the car to avoid a fox that ran in front of the car. "However, I still favor the theory that the killer was trying to stop the production for some reason."

I was thinking. "There must be easier ways to stop a show being produced than murdering someone. And it didn't work, anyway. They're going ahead with the production."

"Really?"

"Yes. I was surprised myself. But Teddy is determined to complete the project, and Molly seems equally keen. This show's a big part of promoting his new book. And Molly seems like the kind of person who finishes what she starts. They've got next weekend already booked to finish shooting."

He looked confused. "But what about Enid?"

"Nobody outside the production will ever know that Enid was originally part of the show."

"They're replacing her?"

"Yes. Teddy chose the replacement. Her name is Margot Dodeson. She's a rather timid woman and Teddy took a shine to her. It was his idea that ask her to replace Enid. She's another one of my customers. An excellent knitter already. And, best of all for Teddy, she's not the type of person who keeps interrupting the class."

He glanced at me significantly. "What a stroke of good luck for Teddy."

I understood his meaning but immediately dismissed it. "I can't believe Teddy would resort to murder just to get a different person in his class."

"What about Margot Dodeson? If she was enamored of Teddy, perhaps she killed Enid Selfe in order to take her place?"

It wasn't a bad thought. "But how could she possibly have known she'd be chosen?"

"Perhaps Teddy whispered in her ear and said, 'Oh, Margot Dodeson, how I wish that you were in my class instead of Enid Selfe.'"

"And then she made it happen." Margot had definitely seemed starstruck by Teddy. But when I'd spoken to her earlier today, she hadn't seemed as though she were expecting the call. Still, Rafe was right. It was too early to dismiss any theories, no matter how outlandish, until we'd explored them.

We motored along for a few more miles. The early evening sun drizzled between the trees that met overhead, throwing patterns of shadow on the road ahead. Idly, I thought how pretty the shadows would look translated into lace. Ha. I was thinking about knitting outside of shop hours. This had to be progress.

Rafe broke the silence. "This won't do your shop any good, having a murder victim found there."

"I know. But the police aren't releasing much about the murder, including the exact location of where it happened."

"That's good news for you. And the television production."

"Poor Enid. She so wanted to be a star. Now she's been written right out of the show."

"Don't waste your sympathy. I suspect that Enid was the author of her own misfortune."

"She certainly did seem to leave a trail of unhappy people behind her."

"One of them was unhappy enough to kill her."

CHAPTER 13

he call of a peacock is not nearly as pretty as the peacock itself. It sounds like a combination between a crow, a seagull, and a honking goose. Long and wailing and weirdly nasal, considering peacocks don't have nostrils.

I could hear their cries as we drew into the drive that led up to Rafe's manor house. It was beautiful. A gardener was training an unruly climbing rose onto a trellis against the ancient wall that edged the gardens that bordered the drive. On one side, three peahens were picking away at the velvet green lawn, taking absolutely no interest in the two peacocks on the other side of the drive, their tails fanned out, the feathers glowing iridescent emerald and sapphire in the sunlight. The peahens might not be impressed by the sight, but I certainly was. Rafe pulled into a modern garage hidden behind a stone wall, and as we emerged, my old friend Henri came waddling up, looking for tidbits.

"Henri, if you get much fatter, you'll end up on someone's table," Rafe scolded the peacock, who was eyeing him, looking for a treat. Nyx took one look at the bird and stalked down toward the front entrance of the manor. Nyx wasn't the kind of cat to use the back door.

"You'd eat a peacock?" I asked in horror.

"It was quite a delicacy in my day. Henri would have been the centerpiece of the feast."

Perhaps Henri knew he was safe, for he seemed to take little interest in Rafe's warning. He regarded me with his black, glistening eyes and fanned his tail out for me. "If I were a peahen, I would marry you in a minute," I told him, delighted as he began to turn in a slow circle, letting me see his full magnificence. I held up my hand, showing him the pellet of bird food I'd taken from the bag Rafe kept in the car. He very delicately took it from my palm.

Rafe took my hand and led me toward the house. Behind me, Henri let out his very unappealing cry. I wasn't sure whether he was thanking me for the morsel or saying, "That's it? I fanned my tail and danced around for one measly pellet?"

"What about my bag?" I asked, pulling back.

"William will see to it."

By the time we got to the front, the doors were open and William was standing there. He looked the most correct gentleman's gentleman apart from the chef's apron he was wearing. "Lucy," he said, giving me a smile. "It's so lovely to see you. I hope you brought your appetite."

"Just the thought of your cooking makes me hungry," I admitted. Shock hadn't affected my appetite much. I'd eaten a huge breakfast this morning, then tucked into the coffee and sandwiches from Elderflower, and now my stomach seemed to be up for one of William's scrumptious meals.

William said, "I've got a surprise for you." Before he could tell us what the surprise was, we pretty much figured it out when a cultured, Oxford-educated voice called out, "Lucy. Rafe. Very nice to see you. Hope you don't mind us dropping by like this. William said it was all right."

I didn't know about Rafe, but I was delighted to see Charlie and Alice. They came around the side of the manor house. She had a notebook in her hand and was holding swatches of fabric, so it didn't take any use of my supernatural powers to work out that they were here for wedding planning.

Rafe strode forward to shake Charlie's hand. "Not at all. Delighted to see you. Will you join us for dinner?"

I couldn't believe that he hadn't checked with William first. I didn't think William kept a well-stocked pantry for humans, but when I asked him in a whisper if there was enough, he gave a soft chuckle. "I love to cook. Don't worry. There's always enough. Besides, I knew they were coming. I hope you don't mind if dinner's a rehearsal for what we'll serve at the wedding." I could tell he was pleased to have people to cook for, so I let my slight worry go. Instead, I walked forward to hug Alice and Charlie.

Alice held me tight. "I'm so sorry about your horrible day. Are you all right?"

"Yes. But please, let's talk about weddings and not murders." I was so happy to have something good to think about, like their wedding, on this dark day. I told them I'd stay out of their way while they were working out their wedding details, but they both cried out in protest. Alice said, "No. I want your advice, Lucy."

And Charlie just looked relieved. "Really, anything you and Alice decide is fine with me." He glanced at Rafe. "Not really my thing, wedding planning."

Rafe laughed and clapped him on the shoulder. "We'll sit on the terrace like civilized men and have a drink while the ladies sort out the details."

I shook my head at Rafe. "Honestly, your attitudes about women are as old as this manor house." Naturally, he and I both knew they were at least that old, but I was trying to bring his notions more into the modern day. With qualified success, but I'm nothing if not an optimist.

There was general laughter, but I hoped that Rafe took my meaning. And then Alice grabbed my hand and said, "Come on around the back. We're going to have the ceremony in Moreton-Under-Wychwood, but the reception will be in the gardens at the back. I'll show you."

I followed her around the side of the building. There was another gardener back there, and it occurred to me that keeping the grounds was almost as much work as the house itself. It was beautiful, though. In the middle distance, a lake shimmered in the sunshine. Grass fields were dotted with sheep, like so many clouds on a green sky. Since Rafe had no need of sheep that I knew of, I suspected he rented out those fields to a farmer. Maybe he just kept the sheep for their aesthetic value. They certainly were pretty.

Alice followed my gaze. "This is such a beautiful spot. I can't believe Rafe's generosity."

I felt warm inside. I refused to call Rafe my boyfriend—you couldn't have a boyfriend who was half a millennium old—but I had some sort of proprietary interest in him. Some things were probably better without a name.

Naturally, Alice, being Alice, had sketched out a full plan of the garden and where everything was going to go. There was very little for me to do except approve. And I did. She had decided on small round tables dotted throughout the gardens, so people could rest a drink or share an appetizer and then move on and circulate. "I didn't want a formal sit-down dinner. I want our friends to meet and mingle."

Since I knew that at least some of the guests would be vampires, I approved her plan heartily. The fewer set meals, the better. I thought her colors were beautiful. She'd chosen a sophisticated shade of pink that was so pale it was more of a blush, and cream. "With my coloring, I can't wear pure white, so I'm going with antique silk." The fabric swatches were for table linens and I could picture how pretty the tables would look. She had pictures of the flower arrangements she was getting, and they were simple—bud vases on the cocktail tables with a single pink rose in each, and larger floral arrangements in tubs around the grounds and on the terrace.

"What do you want me to wear?" Since she'd asked me to be a bridesmaid, I'd had visions of some hideous gown, but she reassured me immediately. "I was hoping you wouldn't mind wearing something in this same pink. We'll choose the dress together, if that's okay."

It was more than okay. I said, truthfully, "I'll just be happy to see you and Charlie tie the knot. You're so perfect for each other."

"I've always known that, but it took Charlie a little longer to fall in love with me."

I didn't share with her that it also had taken a good dose of love potion to encourage Charlie's somewhat clueless heart to recognize its own needs. But Alice didn't need to know those details. She said, "I've asked Violet to be a bridesmaid too. It's funny. I haven't known you two as long as some of my friends, but when I thought about my wedding, you were the ones I wanted to stand up with me."

On some level, I suspected that Alice recognized it was due to Violet and me that she was getting her happy ending. Though it hadn't been a smooth ride. As someone very smart had said, "The course of true love never did run smooth." Especially not if there were witches involved.

While we wandered around the garden deciding on the best places to hang lanterns, Charlie and Rafe settled themselves on the stone terrace. They could see us, but they also had their privacy. And, for Rafe, complete shade. I said to Alice, with a nod to the folder she was carrying around, "Okay, show me your dress."

She giggled. "I haven't completely decided yet. Can I show you pictures of the two dresses I'm down to?"

"Absolutely." I didn't tell her, but the last time I'd been a bridesmaid, I had to accompany the world's pickiest bride to twelve bridal shops and watch as she tried on approximately 7,000,012 wedding dresses and then dictated that we, the long-suffering bridesmaids, all eight of us, should wear a shade of green that has never been seen in nature. It was the color of Astroturf. Needless to say, it wasn't flattering. However, I was a good sport, and I was prepared to be a good sport now. It was so much easier when I had some say in what I'd be wearing and when the bride had done most of the wedding shopping on her own.

She showed me two photographs torn from magazines of bridal gowns. Both were simple, as suited a garden wedding. One had lace sleeves; the other had pearls on the bodice. No wonder she was torn. They'd both look amazing on her and I told her so.

"I tried them both on, but I couldn't decide."

"Okay. You and I and Violet are all going shopping together. We'll help you choose your dress and get bridesmaid dresses at the same time."

"Are you sure you have time?" For anything that made me think of happy occasions and not a woman being murdered in my shop, I had nothing but time.

"Also, I'm looking forward to a new experience." I tried a wicked grin. "The hen party." Okay, we had something similar back home, a bachelorette party, but for some reason in the UK, they called them hen parties. I was pretty familiar with them in Oxford. Groups of young women would totter around from pub to pub in high heels and short dresses, one invariably in a plastic tiara, a sash that said "Bride" and sometimes a bit of lace curtain simulating a veil.

Alice looked horrified at the idea. "Oh, please no." She

swallowed. "I don't want to be humiliated and hung over for my wedding."

I laughed aloud, then promised we wouldn't humiliate her. However, a woman getting married deserved a send-off from her female friends. She promised to give me a list of women coming to the wedding, and I promised no plastic tiaras. Once we were both satisfied with the arrangement, we went to join the men. Charlie was enjoying an amber pale ale in a glass beaded with condensation. Rafe was sipping red wine.

When we arrived and settled ourselves on the terrace, William came out with a cold silver ice bucket containing a bottle of champagne. "Ladies, champagne?"

I began to laugh. "I do love wedding planning." And, if I knew Rafe, that was going to be a very special bottle of champagne.

William popped the cork and poured four icy glasses of champagne. Even the glasses looked like palace treasures. Once we all had the cold bubbling drinks in our hands, Rafe rose and said, "May I propose a toast? To a couple who found true love in spite of all the many bumps along the way." Here he shot a glance at me and raised one eyebrow, so slightly that only I could see the ironic implication. Okay, so Violet and I had caused a few of those bumps along the way. We'd also helped create that happy ending. He continued, "I wish you a long and happy marriage. Charles and Alice, happiness always."

I echoed, "Charles and Alice. Happiness always."

We sipped the champagne, cold, crisp and bubbly. I thought I could spend my whole life drinking nothing but this beautiful bubbly perfection in a glass that probably cost more than my parents' house.

The attention span of Charlie and Rafe for wedding chat was quite a bit less than that of Alice and mine, so the conversation soon turned to the recent drama. While the news hadn't been shared publicly, everyone on Harrington Street knew about the dead body found in my shop.

Charlie looked at me with concern "How are you holding up, Lucy? Rotten bad luck you had this morning."

I never got tired of British understatement. Finding a murdered woman on the floor of my shop was "rotten bad luck," indeed.

I tried not to shudder as I said, "It was horrible. But, luckily, the police were very quick to come and take care of it all."

"Do they have any leads on who did it?"

The million-dollar question. "I don't think so."

Alice said, "If you want a place to stay for a few days, until Cardinal Woolsey's isn't a crime scene anymore, you're welcome to stay with me."

It was so kind of her. I thanked her and then, trying not to blush, said that I would be staying with Rafe for a day or two. They both looked relieved. Alice said, "You'll be safe here."

I thought I'd be safe in my own bed as well, but I probably wouldn't sleep.

Charlie said, "We met her, of course. The woman who was killed. At the book signing. She was hard to miss. One of those people who draw attention."

It was an interesting way to describe a person, but I understood what he meant. It was as though Enid Selfe sucked in more than her fair share of oxygen in a room. "Sadly, the attention she got wasn't always positive. Still, she was very excited about being on TV."

Charlie said, "I never understand why people want to be on television, especially those reality shows, where they all share the same house or go on dates with a cameraman coming along to record the entire ordeal. I couldn't think of anything worse."

"I think Enid Selfe loved the idea of being on television. She was an excellent knitter, and she thought she was going to be the star of the class. But that turned out not to be true.

Teddy Lamont has a very different style, one I personally love. He's not all about perfection of stitches but has a more organic, joyous approach to color and technique. He's not one to get on a fuss if a person makes a few mistakes. Enid was horrified. Her idea of knitting was perfect stitches following a pattern."

Rafe said, "I think I'm with Enid Selfe on this one. If you're going to do a craft, it's nice to do it properly. Then you can worry about your color and your style."

I said, somewhat snappishly, "Well, we haven't all had as much time to practice as other people."

Like hundreds of years of practice. Naturally, we couldn't debate this particular topic in front of Alice and Charlie, so he merely said, "You know what they say, Lucy, ten thousand hours of practice should give you mastery in most things."

The thought of spending ten thousand hours knitting made my eye twitch. I preferred Teddy Lamont's way.

Alice asked, "How are the other class members taking the news of the murder?"

"Surprisingly well. It was so nice of you to let us use Frogg's Books today. We all sat around in shock, and then of course, the police were there interviewing all of the cast and crew one at a time. Obviously, everyone was shocked, but no one really liked Enid Selfe, so it wasn't as sad as it might have been. I think, deep down, we're all secretly relieved that the show can go on without her."

Charlie seemed quite surprised. "They're going ahead? That's rather cold-hearted, isn't it?"

I shrugged. "You know what they say. The show must go on. Especially when Teddy Lamont has a new book to promote and the production company has already sunk a lot of money into making this show. I suppose, so long as no one knows the details, the television viewing public won't be any the wiser." Charlie was right, though. We were practically going to be knitting over that woman's dead body. Or at least over the spot where she'd died.

Alice glared at Charlie. "It will be good for you to have the shop full of people and life again, Lucy."

"Yes." I was going to have to do something about a new display on the wall. I didn't think I could stand to look at those antique knitting needles anymore, especially now that there was a gaping hole in the arrangement.

CHAPTER 14

*C*harlie sipped champagne, but he looked longingly at his beer. He said, "I was surprised at how different knitters are. I should be used to it by now, I suppose. Alice and you and Violet aren't exactly the typical grandmotherly knitters. Your Gran was that, of course. But the people they chose for the show were all ages. That rugged-looking Norwegian bloke surprised me the most. He looked as though he ought to be working in a butcher shop or driving massive machinery, not sitting knitting socks."

I smiled at his description of Gunnar. "I'm sure that's why the producers chose him." I remembered his short bio without any trouble. "And you're not far off. Gunnar used to work on oil rigs in the North Sea. According to his bio, he took up knitting to help him quit smoking. It's fun to watch him knit with those big work-roughened hands. And his work is excellent." I pictured him knitting away and then had to chuckle. "He's a bit of a perfectionist though. And every time he makes a mistake, he says *lort*. And then he apologizes. Says it means 'excrement.'"

Charlie looked at me in surprise. "Don't you mean *dritt?*"

"I don't think so." The words didn't even sound similar.

Charlie shrugged. "That's odd. *Lort* is Danish for, um, excrement. I know because I used to have a Danish girlfriend. Like your friend Gunnar, although her English was excellent, she cursed in Danish. *Dritt* is the Norwegian term."

Alice looked at him in a slightly offended way. "And did you learn that from your Norwegian girlfriend?"

When Charlie turned on his charming grin, he could take your breath away. "You weren't my first, darling Alice. But I promise you'll be my last."

Then he got up and went over to kiss his fiancée while I puzzled over what he'd said.

"That's odd, isn't it? That Gunnar would curse in Danish?"

Rafe said, "One tends to curse in one's native language."

Since somebody involved with the production was a murderer, anything out of the ordinary was worth noting. "You mean Gunnar might not be Norwegian? Who lies about being Norwegian?"

"I have no idea. Gunnar's certainly a Norwegian name."

But now that we were doubting Gunnar, I remembered something else. "When Annabel mentioned that she had hiked Preikestolen, in Norway, I swear Gunnar didn't know what she was talking about. And then he covered it up by saying he wasn't a hiker. It just seemed odd, that's all."

Charlie was a man who lived more in books than anywhere, but he also had a practical streak. "He didn't know Preikestolen? Lucy, I think you should tell the police about Gunnar."

"I suppose you're right. I just hate feeling like I'm tattling on people in school. Getting them in trouble."

"Well, if you can stop a murderer, it's probably worth being a bit of a telltale."

"Maybe he did lie about being Norwegian, but why on earth

would an oil rig worker from Norway, or possibly Denmark, kill Enid Selfe?"

"That's a question for the police," Charlie said.

"But any time someone is murdered in my shop, I also think it's a question for me." Besides, four brains were better than one. "You can't tell anyone else, but I want you to know exactly how she died." They glanced at each other and both leaned forward. I imagined they'd been very curious about the details and too polite to pry.

Charlie said, "Of course, we'll be discreet."

I told them how I'd gone downstairs this morning and found her with the knitting needles stabbed into her chest.

"Knitters really are a tougher bunch than I'd imagined. And this Gunnar character would have the brute force to kill a woman with steel knitting needles."

"But that's not what killed her." I swallowed and, watching me, Rafe took over the narration.

"She was killed by a blow to the head. The back of her skull was bashed in."

Alice went a bit green and sipped more champagne, but Charlie squinted as though picturing the scene. "With the right weapon, anyone of reasonable strength could kill her or at least knock her senseless and then finish the job."

"Exactly," Rafe said.

"But why do it in my shop? That makes it feel somehow personal. The killer had to arrange to meet her there. It wasn't like they grabbed her on the street or in her house. This was premeditated, and they premeditated on Cardinal Woolsey's."

Rafe pushed his champagne aside and went back to his red wine. Seeing this, Charlie did the same and reached for his beer. Alice and I were most happy with our champagne, and both of us held out our glasses for a refill when William came out with hors d'oeuvres.

He said, "I've been experimenting with a few things that I

thought might be nice for your wedding. I've got a whole list of ideas that we can go over, Alice, when it's convenient."

Alice nearly choked on her champagne. "William, you don't have to cater our wedding. I'm hiring caterers."

William shook his head. "I've discussed it with Rafe. It's part of our wedding gift to you, if you'll accept it. Of course, I quite understand if you'd rather have another caterer. But I don't get much chance to use my talents. I'd be very grateful for the opportunity."

Poor man, he really looked like he wanted to do this. Alice smiled at him in gratitude. "Thank you, William. I have to admit it seems such a daunting task to find the right caterer. You'd be perfect."

William also looked pleased. "Wait until you've eaten, then you can decide."

I looked at what was on that tray and thought that if I ever got married, William was going to be my go-to caterer. He offered the tray around, starting with Alice. "These are traditional potato latkes with smoked salmon. The Italian mayonnaise is my own recipe. Beside that are tiny Yorkshire puddings with rare roast beef. There's a selection of fresh shellfish, each with its own sauce. The crepes are vegan, as are the gazpacho and chilled pea soups." The soups were in shot glasses, and his presentation was gorgeous. There were tiny shepherd's pies, a personal favorite of mine, and mini savory scones. He brought out a plate of cheeses, charcuterie and breads to round it all out.

After we'd happily pigged out, Alice formally accepted his and Rafe's generous offer.

"Good. That's settled then. I've got lots more ideas and recipes. We can get together when you're ready and make up a proper menu."

While we nibbled on wedding delicacies, Rafe said, "I've asked Theodore to drop by later."

Charlie glanced up. "Theodore the scenery painter?" Of course, that's how he'd know Theodore. The multitalented vampire helped paint sets when the Cardinal College drama department put on its theatrical performances. But Theodore was also a private investigator. In life, he'd been a policeman, long before the invention of computers, forensics, or CSI. He was old-school, and he was excellent at what he did.

If he hadn't been sleeping all day, he might even have some new information for us.

It was a lovely evening. When William brought out tiny cupcakes with C and A piped on them in icing, Charlie took one and, before he bit into it, said, "We've determined that Gunnar might not be quite the man he'd have us believe. Tell us about the rest of the knitters. Alice and I met them all, the night before that woman was murdered, so perhaps we saw something or we'll remember something."

I glanced at Rafe, who nodded. Nyx came padding up from the garden, looking pleased with herself. She sniffed all the corners of the terrace, and woe betide any mice who might be hiding there, but she appeared satisfied that we were in a mouse-free zone. With the satisfied yawn of a cat who's been busy on secret feline business, she jumped up into my lap, circled a few times and settled herself for sleep. I managed to reach into my bag without disturbing Nyx and pulled out the sheet of bios. I had them nearly memorized by now, but I didn't want to overlook the tiniest fact. I recapped what we knew of Enid and Ryan.

"Vinod is next on the list."

Alice said, "I spoke to him at the book signing. Vinod seemed very nice. I can't imagine he has anything to do with all of this."

"You wouldn't think so. I would say he had the least to do with Enid. He's mostly kept to himself."

"What do we know about him?" Charlie was obviously

becoming interested in this amateur sleuthing business. I suspected in his wide range of reading, he'd consumed many a murder mystery. As though he'd read my mind, he chuckled. "Well, it's rather like one of those classic mysteries, isn't it? Dorothy L. Sayers, Margery Allingham, or even our old friend Agatha Christie. The room of suspects. All seemingly unconnected, but the deeper you dig, the more connections exist. Rather like underground roots that aren't apparent from the surface, not until you get your shovel and do some dirty digging."

He was right, of course. What did I know about Vinod? I thought back on our conversations and read over the brief bio. "He was born in India, but he lives near Birmingham now. He's a radiologist."

"Well, somebody who knows about the human body would certainly know where to maneuver a couple of needles into a person's heart."

It was a good point. It couldn't be easy to bypass the ribs. Perhaps a medical background would've helped. "But again, where's the connection? Was Enid Selfe hitting on him?" I asked. I'd definitely noticed her going after Rafe, but strangely, other than that, I hadn't kept up with her movements.

Alice said, "I don't think so. He seems like a devoted family man. He's terribly proud of his son, his eldest. The boy's seventeen and has been accepted into medical school here in Oxford."

Rafe looked to me. "Didn't you say earlier that Enid Selfe was hoping one of her daughters would go to Oxford?"

"Yes, but they live in Stow-on-the-Wold. How would they know someone from Birmingham?"

Rafe pulled out the printout of the bios and said, "Not Birmingham. It says on the bio that he lives 'near Birmingham.'"

"Oh my gosh, you're right." I couldn't believe I'd been so

sloppy. "He mentioned the name of the town. I just kept reading 'near Birmingham,' and that's what got stuck in my head." I glanced around. "I'm not from here. What towns and villages are near Birmingham?"

They all looked at each other. Alice asked, "Leamington Spa? Coventry?"

"No."

Charlie said, "Castle Bromwich?"

"Yes." I snapped my fingers, making Nyx start. "That one. How did I not remember that? It had the word castle in it."

Charlie asked, "Really? I had quite a long chat with a woman named Helen. She told me she taught science for some years in a posh school in Castle Bromwich."

Wow, those roots were already being uncovered, just with a casual chat over a glass of champagne and canapés. And cupcakes. I leaned forward and chose one. "In the same way these letters are piped together so they connect, maybe Helen's connected to Vinod? Maybe she taught his son?" Not that I had any idea what that had to do with Enid Selfe, but it was a connection.

However, Charlie was already shaking his head. "Most unlikely. She taught at Castle Bromwich *Ladies'* College."

"No boys?"

"No boys."

"Still, it's possible they know each other somehow. She taught in the same place where Vinod lives. And Castle Bromwich can't be a big city."

"Undeniable. It's on the outskirts of Birmingham, I think. But what's the connection with Enid Selfe?"

Alice reached for a second cupcake, and I thought if William was angling for the wedding cake as well, he was hired. "I went to a girls' boarding school. We often had events with a similar school for boys."

She had all our attention now. She blushed slightly. "Well,

isn't it possible that if Vinod's son is going to Oxford that he went to a fancy boys' school? And maybe through the schools having shared events, Vinod met Helen."

"Good thinking, Alice," Charlie said. She went quite pink with pleasure at the compliment. Then he looked at me. "And if that's true, it's very odd that they haven't mentioned that they know each other. Still, I suppose that's a bit weak to pass on to the police, isn't it?"

"It is. But maybe I can find out more the next time the group gets together. There's a lot of time to chat when you're knitting. I'll simply ask some innocent questions and see what I can find out."

"Excellent idea, Lucy."

"Be careful," Rafe said. "Enid Selfe didn't plunge those needles into her own heart."

CHAPTER 15

The amateur sleuthing didn't seem so much fun after Rafe's buzzkill of a comment. After an awkward silence, Alice changed the subject. No doubt handling difficult social situations was a subject they taught at places with names like Castle Bromwich Ladies' College. "I can picture our friends and families mingling in this beautiful garden, waiters circling with plates of food and drinks." She glanced at me. "It's going to be magical."

"It will be," I promised. I knew about magical, and I was determined that I would practice up some spells in case any extra magic was needed. Charlie and Alice deserved an enchanted wedding.

When William came out to offer coffee, we three mortals heaped compliments on him for the amazing delicacies he'd created. The poor man drank in our praise the way a parched and drooping plant drinks water.

The engaged couple didn't stay too long after dinner. After they'd left I said, "You need to give William more humans to cook for. It makes him so happy."

Rafe raised his eyebrows. "Perhaps you should spend more

time here."

So not where I was going with that comment. Fortunately, I was saved from fumbling some sort of answer when Theodore wandered onto the terrace. He'd come round the side of the house, making no noise whatsoever. "Good evening, Lucy. Good evening, Rafe," he said formally.

"Hi, Theodore," I said. Rafe merely nodded at him.

"I'm very sorry about the death in your shop," he said. He didn't add the "again," but it was implied.

"Thank you."

"I've made some progress in looking into this case. Not much, but a little."

"You have? You're amazing. That woman is barely cold."

He cast his eyes to the ground, looking bashful. "I have a lot of time."

Rafe said, "Were you able to discover anything useful?" That was the trouble with sleuthing. So much of it was finding and then eliminating false clues and dead ends. Frustrating work, but necessary.

"I don't know," he answered Rafe. "I've been looking into Enid Selfe's husbands and, um, other significant relationships, as you asked me to."

I'd been so focused on the knitting class and the production crew that I hadn't really thought too much about people in the woman's personal life. "You think it could've been one of the husbands?"

Rafe was leaning back on the parapet, his long fingers resting lightly on the stone. He had a way of looking relaxed and alert at the same time. "What you have to remember about murder, Lucy, is it's rarely an act committed in the heat of the moment. Or even if it is, the seeds have usually been planted long before."

I thought of hot, angry words and violent deeds soon regretted. But when I thought about it, I could see what he meant.

"You're saying that one of her husbands, perhaps, was betrayed by her and over the years has just grown more bitter?"

"It's possible." He glanced at Theodore. "But is it likely?"

Theodore carried a tablet computer with him, but he also had file folders containing notes written in pen. He opened a file folder and took out some notes, but he barely looked at them. "Enid Selfe was born Enid Williams, December 12, 1970. She was married three times. Her first husband, Timothy Fielding, was a junior clerk in a bank. They'd known each other in school, and when he returned from university, they married and had a daughter, Amelia, who is now seventeen years of age. They lived a fairly modest life in London. Mr. Fielding rose very slowly in the banking world."

I made a rude noise. "She thought she'd married Richard Branson and found herself shackled to Mr. Bean?"

"I believe it was something like that, Lucy. And then she met Horace Crisfield. He was an older man and a great deal wealthier. She'd already begun social climbing. She joined a charity to promote literacy in schools. It seems Enid joined organizations in order to meet wealthy men. She was on the board for a medical charity in the hope of meeting a doctor."

"I've heard about people like that but never really believed they were real."

Rafe looked at me a little sadly. "I'm sorry to say they exist. In both sexes."

Theodore cleared his throat, which silenced Rafe and me. "Enid Fielding, as she was then, and Horace Crisfield, who was a married man, began an affair, and she soon became pregnant."

"Seriously?" What was it with this woman and pregnancies?

"It was a bit of a scandal at the time, as he was a rising man in the government. But he did the right thing, or so he told his colleagues, and he left his wife and married the now-divorced Enid Fielding."

"You said she was pregnant?"

"Yes. She had another daughter, Guinevere, now twelve years old. The family moved to Stow-on-the-Wold. She sent both girls to boarding school as soon as they were old enough. She continued her social climbing and, it seems, she wasn't entirely satisfied with Horace Crisfield."

"What a surprise!"

Theodore ignored my outburst and consulted his notes. "It seems she was dissatisfied with the house and undertook a large-scale renovation." In his dry tone, he continued, "She began an affair with the building contractor, Michael Vincent. I haven't uncovered the details, but the marriage ended."

I glanced at Rafe. "That sounds like the seeds of a deep betrayal that could make a man violent. First Horace Crisfield left his first wife because Enid was pregnant, and then after he does the 'honorable' thing, she does a completely dishonorable thing and betrays him with another man."

I glanced at Theodore, feeling like we might have cracked the case already. "Does Horace Crisfield have an alibi for last night?"

"The best alibi a man can have. He's dead."

"Darn it." And why was his name so familiar? "What did he do in the government?"

"He was a senior bureaucrat in the immigration department."

I snapped my fingers. "That's it. Of course." Maybe Horace was dead, but I thought he still might have something to do with his ex-wife's murder. "I heard his name mentioned when Enid and Annabel arrived at the book signing together. They were having a strained conversation the way two strangers have when they're sort of stuck together. They must have met outside on the street and walked in together. Anyway, I overheard Enid tell Annabel that her ex-husband worked for the immigration department."

I closed my eyes and recalled the scene. I could see Annabel's face clearly in my mind. She'd suddenly stiffened. "I'm sure that Annabel asked her to repeat her husband's name, as though she might know it. She looked sick. Her people are from Jamaica, and there was that awful Windrush scandal not so long ago."

Theodore watched me intently. "I haven't begun looking into the class participants, but I can."

Nyx jumped off my lap, and, following her lead, I stood and stretched. "I don't know. Just because Annabel's family originated in Jamaica, doesn't mean she was caught up in the Windrush scandal."

Theodore made a careful note. "I'll put her name at the top of the list and see if I can find any connection between her or anyone in her family and Horace Crisfield."

I still wasn't satisfied. "Would Annabel really have killed Enid because her ex-husband had deported her grandfather or something?"

Rafe said, "With Horace being dead, maybe Enid was as close as she could get. Punishment by proxy."

Theodore went back to his notes. "Enid Selfe was now in her forties and began visiting a plastic surgeon." He allowed himself a little smile. "It seems she began an affair with her plastic surgeon."

I couldn't help it. I laughed out loud. "Of course she did. She bagged her doctor."

"She did. Dr. Liam Selfe."

"Don't tell me, he nipped and tucked her until she figured she could use her new looks to trade up."

"To a football player. Antonio Herrera."

The name meant nothing to me, since I didn't follow sports in the UK. About the only thing I knew was that football in the UK was what we called soccer. "How come she didn't marry him? Did he wise up to her?"

"No. Mr. Herrera sustained a career-ending knee injury."

"And Enid dumped him?"

"She did."

"Maybe he was so bitter and broken-hearted that he killed her." I could imagine that losing a career, a knee and the woman you loved could make somebody crazy.

"I'm still trying to track down Mr. Herrera's whereabouts, but I think it's possible he returned to Spain."

"Who was her prospective fourth husband? There must have been one."

Theodore nodded. "I haven't found out too much about him. He is the newest and the most difficult to learn about. He's minor royalty, with a great deal of private wealth. He seems a very private person, keeps his distance from people."

I had to ask, "What was he doing with her? You'd hardly call her reticent. She told all of us around the knitting table all her business, from the baby she gave up to the many marriages she's had."

Theodore nodded. "It does seem to be an odd match. Still, I can confirm that they'd seen each other a few times."

"Money and a title. She was a determined woman."

"I believe she was a woman who always set her sights higher. Whatever rung of the ladder she was on, she was looking to the next one up," Rafe said in a dry tone. I had the feeling he'd come across people like this in his life. Probably many times. That was one thing about living so long—there wasn't much in human nature he hadn't seen or experienced.

Theodore nodded. "I tend to agree with you. Of course, there are the other dalliances between the marriages, but when she married, she married up."

"She sure kept busy," I couldn't help but remark.

I traced my fingers around the stem of my now-empty champagne glass. "She was always moving on. These men must have realized that she wasn't the sticking type, and yet, they married her. Maybe there was somebody who wanted to marry her so badly that they went kind of crazy. Like, if he couldn't have her, nobody could."

Rafe nodded. "Or it was one she did marry who was enraged that she'd left him."

Theodore looked somewhat perturbed. "Lucy, I can't recall the last time I had this many suspects to investigate for a single crime."

"I know. The trouble with Enid Selfe was that nearly everyone who ever met her had a reason to want her dead."

Rafe nodded. "Back in my more...bloodthirsty days, we used to say that sometimes following our instincts left the world a better place."

I shivered slightly but then reminded myself he was from a different time and different world. He seemed to fit so well into modern society, though there was always that slight edge. He said that old embers could suddenly spring to life, and the person who'd been merely resentful suddenly became murderous. Could it also be true for him? Was it possible that this veneer of civilization covering the bloodthirsty animal part of him was only a thin veil? I wondered what it would take to provoke the vampire. I wondered and hoped I would never find out.

I OPENED my shop as usual on Wednesday. It worked out well, as my customers had expected me to be closed on Tuesday anyway for filming. In fact, we'd been closed due to Cardinal Woolsey's being a crime scene, but that wasn't known outside of Harrington Street. And we Harrington Street retailers tended to stick together. I trusted that no one would blab my unfortunate news.

Once the police had finished, my downstairs neighbors had

helped get rid of the carpet and scrub the plank floor beneath. Theodore arrived with the perfect rug, and then the vampires helped me put my shop back to rights. The film people would turn it back into a set again this coming weekend, but for now, we were back to being a wool shop.

It was a relief to find my normal customers coming in with no clue that when they walked across the middle of the floor, they stepped where a dead woman had lain. I found myself stepping around that area. I didn't know whether it was my perfectly human horror or my witchy senses, but I felt a cold space where the dead woman had lain, and even going too near it made me feel dark and sad.

When Violet came into work and saw me walking around that bad space, she said, "Lucy. Stop this."

I shook my head at her. "I can't. Some part of Enid Selfe's spirit is trapped here in the shop. Do you feel it?"

Violet closed her eyes and took a breath, and as she let it out, she nodded. "You're right. We need to release her. Annoying as she was, her spirit needs to move on." Unlike me, she seemed quite pleased at finding essence of dead woman among the mohairs and the alpacas. I soon found out why. "We'll need Margaret Twigg and my grandmother, and together we'll do a spell that will set the dead woman's spirit free."

I knew that the four of us together created a very powerful energy, but I was nervous about what that energy might do. "You're sure? All we are going to do is release this poor woman's spirit? Nothing can go wrong?"

"Lucy, we're your sisters. You need to have more faith."

She was right, I knew. It wasn't only faith in the other witches that I lacked, but faith in myself and my own powers. Because I'd come to witching so late, it was as uncomfortable as trying to converse in a new language. I always thought I was going to slip up, say or do the wrong thing. She said, "We'll come tonight, just before midnight. Be ready for us."

I might have argued, but the door opened and Margot Dodeson walked in. I thought she walked a little straighter and stood a little taller now that she'd been chosen for the show. She'd done something different with her hair. Lightened it and had it styled. Even her dress looked new. I was so pleased I'd been the one to make that phone call. "Margot, how nice to see you. I like your new look."

She blushed with pleasure at the compliment. "I was so thrilled to get your phone call. I'm here, as you can imagine, to pick up my wool and needles so that I can get caught up before Sunday. I'll practice, of course, before I even attempt to work on anything on television."

"You don't need to practice. Teddy will tell you everything you need to know."

She shook her head. "It is such an honor to be chosen to be on the program, I don't want to let him down. Isn't he the most wonderful man?"

"He is." It was nice to see her genuine excitement at being part of this program. The excitement we'd all had before tragedy had struck. I gave her the new package with her name on it that would contain an assortment of wools and a guide to lace knitting. However, she insisted she wanted to start something else before opening her kit. Since she had her proof copy of Teddy's book, she'd already chosen the pattern she wanted to make. It was a beautiful lace sweater, and she chose a lovely shade of teal, which fortunately, I had in stock from Larch Wools. She walked straight to the side wall where the wools were kept, not bothering to browse the shop. She went away so happy that I thought she'd bring some genuinely nice new energy to Teddy's class.

And we needed new energy quite badly.

But first, I needed to get rid of that bad energy that was making my shop so depressing.

CHAPTER 16

*W*hen we closed, I went upstairs and opened the glass case where Gran had kept some of her special books. I'd added a few of my own, and tucked away in its accustomed spot was the family grimoire. I kept it spellbound at all times now, since the book of magic had almost been stolen. Once I released the book from its spell, I sat on the couch and opened the cover. As soon as Nyx smelled it, she jumped up beside me. I knew she was my familiar, but she was also my pet and my comfort. "We need a spell to send poor, dead Enid Selfe on her way. Too much of her essence is stuck in the shop."

Nyx's head bobbed up and down. It was easy to imagine she was agreeing with me when she was just doing regular cat behavior. Then I realized she hadn't been in the shop all day. "You felt it too, didn't you? We're going to try and release her tonight." I flipped through the book until I found the spell that I wanted. Then I made a list of the ingredients we needed: sage; black and white candles, a lot of herbs I knew Gran had grown in the garden. Since it was summer, most of those herbs were fresh for the picking. I had always assumed she had such a well-stocked herb garden because she liked to cook, but what she liked to cook up was spells. And now it was my turn.

Nyx wandered out with me as I made my way into the herb garden. I picked them fresh and then carried the herbs upstairs with me. I'd picked fresh sage, but really it should be dried and bundled so it could be burned to smoke out bad energy and spirits. Both Gran and Margaret Twigg had encouraged me to keep my supplies stocked and ready at all times and I felt bad I hadn't listened. I hung the sage to dry, even though it wouldn't be ready in time.

I needed to up my game I realized as I looked through Gran's stash of candles. I needed pure beeswax candles and black candles. I dug out the last of the black candles and began making a shopping list. I was a witch, I had to start acting like one and be more prepared.

Before Rafe could show up to drive me back to his place, I texted him to let him know what was up and that I'd be spending the night here.

He texted back. "I'll wait downstairs until you're ready to leave."

I might have argued, but while I'd been sitting here with Nyx, I'd felt the cold, bad feeling start to creep upstairs and into my home. It reminded me of the time a rat had died in the walls of our house in Boston and we'd only known about it as the smell began to permeate the whole house. Enid Selfe's remaining spirit was the psychic equivalent of a decomposing dead rat. Until I was certain she was gone, I really didn't want to stay here.

Besides, William had cooked me breakfast this morning. Eggs Benedict on a savory scone with coffee from a fancy machine that ground the beans fresh for each cup. It wasn't exactly a hardship to stay at Rafe's.

With no William to cook me dinner, I looked in my fridge and cupboards, which were distressingly bare. I had half a dozen tins of the tuna Nyx liked. I opened one for her and then, with a shrug, opened a tin for myself. I had half a loaf of bread in the freezer, so I toasted a couple of slices, spread some mayo on the toast and tried not to compare the uninteresting tuna fish sandwich with the gourmet fare of the night before.

Then, with a sigh, I decided to catch up on paperwork. In spite of murders, television shows, and a rather complicated love life, I still had a business to run.

Just before midnight, I headed down to my shop with all the supplies and my grimoire, feeling unaccountably nervous that it was so late and I was once more alone in the shop with Enid. Well, Nyx was with me, but her eyes were wide, and she was so skittish, she made me worse.

I really wanted Enid out of my shop. I hadn't liked her in life, and I didn't like her any more in death. Even though her death was tragic, her aura was sticky and unpleasant, like an oil stain on the driveway or gum that catches on the bottom of your shoe and won't let go. I couldn't wait to get rid of her.

One thing I will say about my local witches, they were prompt. At exactly eleven-fifty, Violet, Margaret Twigg, and my great-aunt Lavinia knocked on the door. I'd contemplated asking Gran to join us, but I was worried that her energy had changed too much when she had moved from witch to vampire. I had a feeling that for this kind of a spell, we needed pure witch power.

Margaret Twigg entered first. She tended to do that, as though she were the queen and everyone else should fall back in line. Naturally, since she could turn you into something unspeakable at the snap of a finger, we tended to let her go first.

She walked in holding a small cauldron and a black bag that bulged. I didn't entirely trust Margaret Twigg; the last potion she'd brewed for me had been a love potion that went terribly wrong. Still, it hadn't completely been her fault, and at least we couldn't do harm to someone who was already dead. Could we?

She no sooner stepped in the shop than she recoiled as though she smelled something horrible. "Oh, dear, I can see why you need us. That murder victim has not moved on."

I was pleased that she could feel it too and it wasn't overactive imagination on my part. She walked unerringly to the exact spot where Enid had died and looked down, almost as though she could see the poor woman lying there dead. "Right. You'll make sure we aren't disturbed?"

I'd spoken to the vampires downstairs and could assure her that we'd have the place to ourselves.

She nodded briskly. "Good."

Nyx stayed right beside me. Margaret had catnapped her once, and my cat was wary of her. Understandably.

I discovered that everything didn't have to be magic. Margaret Twigg had bought along a small camping stove. On it, she placed the small cauldron. From her capacious black bag, she pulled out a bottle of what I assumed was distilled water and poured it into the cauldron.

I showed her the herbs I'd brought in from the garden. The bundle of sage looked like greens that had been in the bottom of the fridge too long. She looked at the floppy, sad bundle and shook her head. "Really, Lucy. You must always be prepared."

Then she pulled out two fat bundles of dried sage and one of lavender and three small bottles.

However, after dissing my fresh sage, she looked at the rest of the herbs carefully. "Are these the ones Agnes grew?"

"Yes."

"Harvested today?"

I nodded.

"Fine." She nodded. "Clover, asafetida, we just want a little, and some nettle and, perhaps a pinch of the rosemary." She took the herbs and threw them into the cauldron with the liquid. She added several drops from the tiny bottles and I smelled basil, then the licorice scent of anise. "The steam will help cleanse the space. Everything we do is about taking solid and turning it to air, light enough to float away."

I arranged the candles in a circle around where Enid Selfe had died. First a ring of the black, to draw out the bad energy, and then around it, a ring of beeswax candles to purify and send the energy on its way.

I watched Margaret Twigg carefully. When the cauldron was boiling and the scent of herbs began to fill the air, she pulled out a small vial of white crystals. As she was about to shake them into the cauldron, I grasped her wrist. "What is that?"

"Salt."

I leveled my gaze steady on hers. "What kind of salt?"

"Salt from the Dead Sea. It helps purify the spirit and ease them on their way."

I wasn't some rube at a country fair. "Salt from the Dead Sea? Are you sure you didn't buy a one-pound sack of table salt from Tesco's?"

Her lips twitched, and I could see her trying not to laugh. "All right, probably ordinary table salt would do just fine, but I use the best. Now stand back." She glanced down at my hand, and her voice went steely. "And let go of my arm."

I did and stepped back. Luckily I did, for the second she shook the salt into the pot, the boiling became furious.

"Lavinia? The candles, if you please."

Lavinia focused hard and then snapped her fingers, and the candle wicks all sprang into flame at once. It was so cool, I was determined to start practicing that spell on my own.

She said, "Now, witches, we join hands." We circled around the space where Enid Selfe died. We stood outside the ring of fire, which, I knew from my grimoire, was to protect us from the negative energy. The cauldron bubbled away in the very spot where Enid had died, and the candles circled the spot. The flames should act like a psychic chimney, channeling Enid's leftover energy away from us. I had Violet's hand holding my left and Margaret Twigg's clawlike grasp on my right hand. Lavinia closed the circle, joining with Margaret and Violet, and Nyx sat beside me, her soft warmth against my ankle. And then Margaret looked at me. "Lucy? Please take over."

I felt like a brand-new intern being handed a scalpel during brain surgery.

They were all looking at me. I felt panic rise. I said to Margaret, "Can't you do it?"

She smirked in an entirely superior fashion. "Of course I can do it. But you need to practice in order to learn. Besides, this is your shop, and you're the one who has the most to lose if we don't get rid of the spirit."

I glanced at Lavinia, who merely nodded. Violet squeezed my other hand and whispered, "You've got this."

Easy for her to say. She was just an hourly paid employee. If Enid started creating havoc in my shop, all Violet had to do was quit. Me? I was stuck in this place. It was my place of employment, I lived above the shop, and don't even get me started on the beings living below who seemed to think it was my job to keep them safely housed.

But, on some level, I also knew that Margaret Twigg, as annoying as she was, was probably right. I looked around at their faces, strangely almost unrecognizable in the flickering candlelight. "What if it goes wrong?"

"Then you'll know that you're not trying hard enough. Being a witch isn't like learning to needlepoint or to paint watercolors, Lucy, this is a vocation. If you don't take it seriously, somebody's going to get hurt, and that somebody is probably you."

"Great pep talk. Thanks. Now I feel full of confidence."

"This potion won't stay strong forever. You're wasting time."

I took a deep breath. I brought back that sense I'd had when I was feeling powerful as I read my family grimoire. I pictured the handwritten spell that I'd memorized. I pictured Enid Selfe's face. My fingertips began to tingle, not the kind of tingling that ended up in shooting flames; the feeling of inner power. The handwritten verse had been a poem, with antiquated words that rhymed. I felt I wanted something simpler. I improvised my own spell, hoping Margaret would fix things if I made a mess of it.

"We sisters have come together. North, South, East and West. Fire, air, earth, and water. As four elements, four directions, four sisters. Together, we exhort you, spirit of the departed, to rise and go on your way. Your time here on earth is done. It is time for you to rise and go on your way." I couldn't think of anything else, so I added the words that ended the spell. "So I say, so mote it be."

I felt a kind of electric current running between me, Margaret, and Violet. There was absolute silence. The candle flames burned steadily. Was I supposed to say more? I didn't have anything more.

I was about to ask Margaret to take over when, suddenly, the water boiled, faster and louder than normal water could boil. It sounded like a waterfall, and the steam rose and circled about. Violet gasped and clutched my hand so hard, I think she broke a couple of small bones.

The column of steam suddenly became Enid's face, if Enid had been made of steam. In a shrieking tone, she said, "Find out who took my life from me, or I will be back."

I might be completely freaked out, but I was also an amateur sleuth. I wasn't going to give up any chance to find the answer to this puzzle, and who knew better than Enid herself who'd killed her? "Enid, do you know who hurt you?"

She shrieked again and began to spin. Honestly, if I hadn't been clutching two other witches, I'd have turned tail and run all the way upstairs to my flat, thrown myself in my bed, and pulled the covers over my face.

Enid cried out, "Danger comes to this place. Death comes."

She made another of those unearthly shrieking sounds, and then the column of smoke, steam, or whatever it was began to spin.

Before my astonished gaze, it began to ricochet around the room. Suddenly she screamed again, "Let me out!"

Margaret Twigg seemed to jump out of the trance. "Open the door," she screamed. I ran to the door, stumbling in my haste, while Enid's ghost tore around my shop, shrieking. Finally, I got the door open, and with a final howl, she flew out into the night. The other three witches crowded behind me, and we burst out of the door and onto the sidewalk. All of us looked up. What began as a tight column of vapor dissipated so fast, I could've believed I'd imagined it. And then there was nothing.

We walked back inside. The candles were all out. Nyx walked around the outside of the candles and let out a meow. And then she walked around the perimeter of the shop sniffing, her tail twitching.

Margaret Twigg looked on approvingly. "She's making sure the spirit's all gone."

I glanced from Nyx to Margaret. "Is it?"

"I think so. I don't feel her essence here anymore, do you?"

I was so stunned, I didn't know what I was experiencing. She said, "Just to be sure, we'll do a final cleansing."

She took one of her fat bundles of sage and lavender, lit it with a snap of her fingers and handed it to me. I walked around the room, waving the smoking sage, calling on the four winds, the four elements, represented here by four witches. It was like sweeping up after the garbage truck had already been through. There wasn't much left, but a few wisps of vapor trailed out my door. Finally, Margaret Twigg nodded. "You've cleansed your space."

"But did you hear what she said? She said if I don't find her killer, she'll be back to haunt me."

"Yes, Lucy. We all heard it."

"What do you think she meant when she said death is here?"

Margaret sounded irritable. "I don't know. Ghosts always talk in riddles. Would it hurt them to give a straight answer to a simple question?"

For once I was in complete sympathy with Margaret Twigg. "I know."

But the space felt lighter, cleaner, fresher somehow. I could take a full breath and not feel Enid.

"Thank you," I said, truly meaning it. "Thank you all for coming."

Margaret Twigg sniffed. "You can show your thanks by offering us a drink."

I looked at them. "Really?"

The three of them nodded. Lavinia sighed. "There's nothing like a good whiskey and soda after dispatching a spirit."

"But it's after midnight. The pubs will be closed."

Margaret took a bottle out of her bag. "You're going to have to stock your liquor cabinet, along with your magic supplies, Lucy. Luckily I came prepared."

Rafe would take me back to his place, but he was probably happily visiting downstairs. I supposed a quick drink wouldn't hurt and it might calm my jangled nerves.

"You did well, Lucy," Margaret said, quietly as we left the shop to go up to my flat. "We'll drink a toast to your success."

Being a witch was full of surprises. Some of them quite good ones. "Okay," I said. "Get rid of the lingering spirit of a dead woman and toast the deed. All in a day's work for the modern witch. Let's go."

CHAPTER 17

he second class that Teddy Lamont hosted was understandably more subdued than the first. There had been some discussion as to whether we should inform Margot Dodeson about her predecessor's unfortunate demise, and, wisely I thought, Molly decided that we should tell her. Not the gory details, of course, but simply that she was replacing a woman who had unfortunately passed away suddenly.

When I'd invited Margot to join us, I'd only said that someone had to drop out. I left it to Molly to tell her that "drop out" in this case was a euphemism for "dead."

Everyone in the class was warned not to say anything more than that. We were, once more, in my shop. The set people had reinstalled the same table and chairs and moved my stock around once more. The only thing a sharp-eyed viewer would notice was that the rug had been changed.

Margot Dodeson couldn't have been more unlike Enid Selfe. Before taking a seat, she looked around and asked where we all liked to sit. Teddy beamed at her and insisted she sit in front, where Enid had sat. That made it easier for the rest of us, as we assumed the same seats we'd sat in the last time we were in this class.

Under Margot's adoring gaze, Teddy became almost as happy as he had the first day when we'd started this class. The shop was so much lighter without Enid, either alive or dead, and I think we all felt the difference. Naturally, we'd had a head start with Teddy and, after he gave a short talk on technique, he said, "I want the rest of you to continue with your knitting. I'm going to take this lovely lady next door. We'll have coffee, and I'll give her the short version of the first lesson."

I thought Margot would die of happiness. "Oh, you don't have to."

He patted her hand. "My dear, you have saved us all." And as he led her away, I thought that he was treating her the way Enid had longed to be treated. If only she hadn't been so awful.

As soon as they were out the door and Molly stopped the filming, the rest of us could gossip in comfort about the topic that was topmost in all of our minds.

No sooner had the door closed on them than Ryan said, "Well? Are there any leads? Does anyone know who killed that old crone?"

"I can tell you one thing, the cops will think it was you if you keep talking like that," Annabel warned him. She turned to me. "Lucy?"

I shook my head. "No. I haven't heard anything." Well, officially, I hadn't.

Vinod said, "I have been watching the news. There is nothing about the poor woman's demise."

Annabel replied, "I imagine the police want to keep the details quiet. They don't want everybody knowing as much as the murderer does. That's how you catch murderers."

Ryan finished a row and flipped his work to start the next. "Look who's been watching too many police dramas on telly."

We all laughed, which let off some tension. Gunnar said, "I

would never have come on this show had I known I would become involved in a murder investigation."

I thought to myself, is your name even really Gunnar? I wished I knew Norwegian so I could trip him up.

Annabel said, "I bet it was one of her husbands. She's had enough of them. Did you notice she never even talked about them? Only her two daughters. She reminded me of the wicked stepmother in Cinderella. Shoving her kids' feet into shoes that didn't fit so long as they could get the prince."

"But first, they had to get into the right schools," Vinod reminded her.

"Maybe her daughters killed her. Can you imagine having that woman as your mother?" Ryan shuddered.

Annabel glanced at him. "You almost did. Last week, she all but claimed you as the baby she gave away."

"Well, I'm not, okay?" He sounded belligerent and angry. Ryan always seemed so easygoing that we all stopped knitting to stare. He stabbed his needle into the next stitch. "Just leave it alone."

After an awkward pause, Helen said, "I don't understand what she was doing here. Why would someone ask Enid Selfe to meet at your shop late at night, Lucy?"

They were looking at me as though I might've lured the woman to her death. I felt my anxiety rise, and so did my voice. "I don't know. I was asleep in bed upstairs when she was killed."

"You live upstairs?" Gunnar asked, gazing up at the ceiling. I could have bitten off my tongue. *Way to go, Lucy. Announce to a room that might contain a murderer that you live here.*

"Not right now," I hastily added. "I'm staying with a friend." And I'd never been so grateful to Rafe as I was at that moment. Of course, I didn't tell them that even after she died, Enid hadn't completely departed. It had taken four witches and some powerful magic to get rid of the woman.

Helen looked quite shocked. "Of course Lucy wouldn't hurt anyone. I believe you're innocent."

That sounded like faint praise. I looked around the table. The production company had put all of them up at the same hotel. While I'd been chatting with William over another decadent home-cooked breakfast this morning, had they been breakfasting together in the hotel talking about me behind my back? Maybe they thought I was the most likely suspect, as the woman had been killed in my shop. I could have borrowed Teddy's phone as easily as anyone else, and with an inward cringe, I remembered I'd been the first to guess his password when the police had asked about it. I looked down the row at the knitters. "Do the rest of you think I killed that woman? Do you want me to excuse myself from being part of this project?"

Helen shook her head. "Of course not. I'm sorry, Lucy. We're all feeling stress. I was thinking aloud."

"I understand." And I did. I was looking at them all like they were killers, too. "Somebody killed her. In order to get to the who, I guess the question is why? What was there about Enid Selfe that caused her to be killed?"

Helen said, "Someone hated her and saw an opportunity. Who knows what secrets she held?"

I looked at Helen. "Secrets? Or was it revenge?"

She paused in her knitting and looked up at me. Her eyes were bloodshot, and there were blue circles of strain beneath. "Perhaps it was both." She went back to her knitting. "I think Annabel's right. The police should check out those husbands."

I had a mission today, and I mustn't forget it. I wanted some more background on these people. I said, "Let's forget about the murder for a few minutes."

As if.

Rafe's words suddenly came back to me. Enid had not stabbed herself in the chest with those knitting needles. Yes, there were many possible suspects, but I couldn't ignore the fact that every single person around this table was pretty handy with the needles.

I glanced around the shop. There were Molly and Becks, both in the corner with laptops, chatting softly, and the cameraman, now munching an apple while checking his phone, and the sound guy, who heard everything.

Helen rose to stretch out her back. "Lucy, if it doesn't work out with your friend, you'd be more than welcome to come and stay with us."

I thanked her, but I wondered if it was a bit like the spider offering the poor unsuspecting fly a nice place to stay for a few days. I would be glad when Enid's killer was caught and I could stop suspecting everybody who came into the shop of being a murderer. It was fatiguing.

I was so busy thinking about murder that I dropped a stitch. However, thanks to Teddy, I just carried right on knowing that the extra hole would add a little personality into the piece. My knitting was full of personality.

With all this color to play with, it was hard for any of us to worry too much about technique. We turned tedium into joy.

Gunnar must've also dropped a stitch, for he muttered *lort* under his breath. I said, trying to sound casual, "Isn't that a Danish curse?" Everyone turned to stare and no wonder. Look at me, knowing how to swear in Danish and, more impressive, being able to tell the difference between Norwegian and Danish swear words. I just hoped no one asked me to speak either language because all I knew were the two curse words.

He looked up from his knitting and blinked at me. His eyes were a cold gray-green like the northern sea, and they certainly chilled me when he stared at me. "I spent many years on Danish oil rigs." He gave a wry smile. "A man learns many Danish curse words when sailing with the Danes."

Okay, that made sense. I mean, look at me. I'd only been living in this country less than a year, and I heard myself saying the strangest British things with my American accent. I'd begun saying "Where's the toilet?" instead of the bathroom, my car had a boot instead of a trunk, and rather than putting trash into cans, I put rubbish into bins. But when I swore, I still did it like an American.

I felt the time running out before Margot and Teddy would return. Molly sent Becks out, and I bet she'd been told to get them back. I turned to Helen, trying to act casual. "And you're a teacher, I believe?" I asked as though I were a hostess at a tea party and it was my job to keep the conversational ball rolling.

She didn't look up from her knitting. "That's right. I teach science. I particularly try to encourage the girls as too few of them continue in the sciences."

"It must be incredibly difficult to teach teenagers. I remember being a teenager, and nobody could tell me anything."

She chuckled. "I think that's why I enjoy my job so much. If you can take a stubborn teenage head and force some knowledge into it, you're doing an acceptable job. But when you see that moment a student gets it—when they begin to ask questions, the right questions—you can see that thirst for learning and you can guide them. Well, then I remember why I became a teacher."

Once again I found myself running against a brick wall. I didn't like to pry into these people's lives, but if I didn't, Enid Selfe might haunt me, and I was going to do anything I could to prevent that from happening. Even if it meant interrogating perfectly innocent people around the knitting table.

"I think I heard you say that you had left a fancy school where the parents pay high fees for a state school. Did you just get tired of all the snobs?"

She kept knitting, but her fingers went rigid. "Something like that."

I was getting sick of this British stiff-upper-lip nonsense. We should move this interrogation to California, where everyone loved to spill their guts.

"What about inheritance?" Ryan asked out of nowhere.

There was dead silence for a second, and then Vinod said, "I beg your pardon?"

"Money." Ryan glanced up and around the table. "Isn't that why most people kill? For money?"

"But Enid had daughters. Her children will inherit her wealth." Helen said and then her eyes widened.

We all stopped knitting and stared at Ryan. What if he really was Enid Selfe's son? I was fuzzy on the laws here, but might he have a claim on her estate if he could prove he was her firstborn son?

I had no idea how rich she'd been. Was her estate large enough to tempt a forgotten son? But what about those girls that were her pride and joy? Could they be in danger from a brother they never knew they had?

He looked around, puzzled. "Why are you all staring at me like that?" And I saw the second he caught up to us. He shook his head and laughed. "Oh, no. Oh, no, no, no. You are not pinning this on me. Enid Selfe couldn't be my mother. At least I hope not. And if she was, I wouldn't want anything from her."

"Easy words to say." Annabel had seemed quite sympathetic to Ryan, but she was also a strong woman making her way in the tough London job market. She didn't waste time being nice. Now we all turned to stare at her. "I'm not saying Ryan killed the woman, only that the police should look into whether he's really her son. We were all here when she said he might be." She turned to him. "And we all heard what you said."

He stared at her. "I can't believe you. I thought we were friends."

Her face was hard. "Matey, if you put the needles in that woman's chest, we'll consider the budding friendship over."

He threw up his hands, and his knitting fell to the floor. "She's not my mother, and I didn't kill her."

"Maybe you didn't mean to kill her. You arranged to meet her here so you could talk but she enraged you so much that you temporarily lost your mind. It could happen."

"Well, it didn't bloody happen to me."

I felt awful for Ryan but impressed with Annabel, who was doing the job I'd intended to do: figuring out who among us had a motive for murder.

CHAPTER 18

$\mathcal{B}$efore Ryan and Annabel started stabbing each other with knitting needles, I took the conversational ball back, determined to learn from Annabel. "Helen," I said with false cheer. "What was it like teaching at a fancy boarding school with all those rich kids?"

She looked cornered and harassed. I felt really bad grilling her since she seemed like a very nice woman—unless she was a killer.

She looked around as though someone might come and rescue her. No one did. Finally she said, "Not much to tell, really. I had some very good students and some not so very good students. I taught there for eight years, and then it was time for a change."

"Why?" I read the newspapers. I knew that England, like many places, was struggling to make education more accessible to all, while the gap between advantaged and disadvantaged students seemed to be growing. Rich people, as they always had, were sending their kids to very expensive schools. Those kids were groomed for the top universities. Boarding schools had prescribed homework times. The kids were expected to excel and offered every possible enrichment to make sure they did. They had debating teams, the most sophisticated and expensive computer labs. If they had a "let's go to work with Mommy or Daddy" day, they'd be shadowing a cabinet minister, a surgeon, a television presenter, or a Nobel Prize-winning geneticist. Meanwhile, funding for state schools was being cut and teacher salaries weren't rising, so good teachers were leaving the system, and fewer young people were going into teaching as a profession. Kids in state schools were falling further and further behind.

Helen patted her colorful lace as though it were an exotic pet. "My current school is closer to home, and state schools are desperate for science teachers."

She came across like a dedicated teacher and a wonderful person, practically a saint. Could she have killed someone?

Playing a sudden hunch, I asked, "Which fancy, posh boarding school did you teach at?"

She shook her head at me like I was that annoying kid at the back of science class who always asked stupid questions and forgot to do their homework. "Lucy, stop calling it that. My school had a proper name. Castle Bromwich Ladies' College. What about that sounds posh or fancy?"

She said the words in such a deadpan way that had I not seen the flash of humor cross her eyes, I never would have believed she was making a joke.

But, joke or no joke, she and Vinod must know each other.

Indeed, he turned to her with amazement. "You taught at Castle Bromwich? But I live there."

She seemed genuinely surprised. "No. Do you really? Obviously, you don't have a daughter in CBLC or I'd have met you by now."

He chuckled. "I hope my daughter will one day go to that fine school, but she is only seven years old. My son goes to Bromwich Grammar School."

"That's an excellent school. How old is he?"

"Seventeen." I could almost see his chest swell with pride. "He has been accepted to medical school here at Oxford." This wasn't the first time he'd shared this news with us, but Helen was too nice to say so.

"That's wonderful. Some of the girls I taught would be about that age now. I wonder what's happened to them all."

I thought it was sweet that she cared. Also, neither she nor Vinod seemed furtive or guilty. In fact, I really believed they didn't know each other. Or they were great liars. The sleuthing business was never simple.

Teddy and Margot Dodeson returned, and for the next hour he went around to each of us inspecting our designs, offering suggestions, and generally treating each knitter as though they were a budding fiber artist. Thankfully, since I was supposed to know what I was doing, he just patted me on the shoulder as he went by and didn't comment on my work.

We broke for lunch at one o'clock. The crew left first while we packed up our knitting. Molly and Becks said they had to return to the hotel for a conference call with London and asked Teddy if he'd be all right. He assured them he would.

The knitters all turned to me expectantly. "Well, Lucy? Where should we go for lunch?"

I liked that the group wanted to be together, but if I'd known that would happen, I could've booked somewhere. I thought rapidly. There were plenty of good restaurants in Oxford, but we didn't have all day. "There's a pub at the top of the road. They've got a nice garden out back. There's quite a range of food."

We looked at Teddy, who was clearly the star of our show. He said, "Yes. Fabulous idea. All right if Douglas joins us?" When everyone agreed, I ushered them out of the front of the store, hanging back so I could lock the door behind them. Vinod, who had the same kind of good manners as Rafe, said,

"I'll walk up with you, Lucy." I imagined he didn't like the idea of leaving me here alone, in case the murderer came back.

Unless he was the murderer. I gulped but knew that all I had to do was call out and some very protective vampires would be up here before I'd finished the scream.

Instead of attacking me, Vinod browsed the wools while I turned off the lights and retrieved my bag with my keys. When we left, a young woman was hovering to one side of the doorway. I'd never seen her before, but there was something vaguely familiar about her. She came forward when she saw me. Her eyes looked swollen and tear-stained. I hoped she wasn't looking for help with a knitting disaster. I had plenty of my own.

I was about to tell her we were closed, but then Vinod asked, "Amelia? What are you doing here?"

"Mr. Patel?" She sounded astonished to see him here.

"My dear, I'm so sorry for your loss."

And then I knew why she looked familiar. She resembled her mother, Enid Selfe.

"I needed to come here, Mr. Patel." Her eyes filled with tears. She took out an already wet and crumpled tissue and wiped her eyes. "The police told me it happened...it happened here."

I was filled with compassion. "Oh, you poor dear. I'm so sorry. You're Enid's daughter?"

She nodded. "I've just been with the police. They told me where it happened but not much else. I just needed to see..."

"Of course." Vinod stepped forward and took her hands. "Amelia. I'm so very sorry."

Whoa. He knew Enid's daughter?

"Thank you." She sounded stunned. "I'm so happy to see you. I never meant—I never wanted—" She inhaled and exhaled a quick breath and some color returned to her face. "How is Ashvin?"

"He's fine. He's fine."

She shook her head. "Mummy only wanted the best for me. She didn't mean to be cruel. You know she threatened to take me out of boarding school and bring me home to finish at our local state school. It would've ruined my chances of getting into a decent college."

He nodded, solemnly. "I know. It's all right."

She looked from him to me. "I was so angry with her, and now she's dead." She began to cry.

Vinod and I looked at each other. Since they obviously knew each other, I said, "Would you come in, too?" She looked like she could use a friend. He nodded, and the three of us went back into the shop, and I turned the lights back on.

I didn't want to tell this poor young woman anything the police hadn't already shared. "What have the police told you?"

She looked around as though she might find her mother hiding in the corner. She shook her head. "They didn't tell us very much. A blow to the back of her head killed her. And it happened in your shop. Of course, they aren't releasing that information to the public, but I assume you know."

"I do." I didn't tell her that I was the one who had found her mother. And it didn't seem that she knew about the knitting needles. Or maybe she couldn't bear to talk about it.

"Your mother was working on a lace cardigan for you. She was so proud of you and your sister. She talked about you a lot."

Her eyes spilled over again. "That's nice. I can't believe it. It just seems impossible that I won't go home for the weekend and find her there. That she won't suddenly turn up at school to make sure they're teaching properly or to argue with them if I don't get high enough marks." I handed her a box of tissues, and she blew her nose on a fresh one. "She always thought it was the teacher's fault if I didn't do well enough. Never that it might have been mine."

"It must be so difficult. Do you have someone you can stay with?"

"My sister and I are staying with our stepfather. But it's not the same. He and Mum were getting a divorce. I'll go back to school as soon as I can after the funeral. It's better if I keep busy."

Vinod said, "You are very brave. When I lost my mother, I was much older than you, but it was still a terrible shock. You must come to the house for dinner. You'd be most welcome."

She wiped her wet cheeks with her hands. "But what about Ashvin? He probably never wants to see me again."

"Nonsense. He's still your friend. We all are."

"Thank you," she said, and then her shoulders began to shake. Before I could move, Vinod took her in his arms and patted her shoulder while she cried against his chest. "There, there," he said soothingly.

I didn't show Amelia the exact spot where mother had fallen, and she didn't ask to see it. After the storm of weeping had subsided, I asked, "Would you like to join us for lunch?" I had no idea if that was inappropriate, but I couldn't send this poor sobbing girl off by herself.

She shook her head. "Thank you, but no. My stepdad and my sister are waiting at the hotel. He thought I was crazy to want to see the spot where she died, but I needed to."

"Of course you did. I understand."

She took a couple of fresh tissues and wiped her cheeks and blew her nose again. "Thank you. You've been very kind."

"You must treat my family like your own."

"Thank you, Mr. Patel. I would love to come for dinner at your house."

"I will tell Ashvin to phone you, and he will arrange it. Whenever you are ready."

"Are you sure he's not angry? She told him I couldn't see

him anymore, and then she got him fired. I'm so ashamed. I should have argued more."

"Amelia, your mother loved you very much, but she was not easy to stand against. You must not worry. We all understand."

After she left, I turned out the lights once more. Vinod waited for me to lock up, and then we headed toward the pub to join the others. My mind was whirling with new conjectures. Vinod's son and Enid Selfe's daughter?

I said, "What a good thing you knew Amelia. You were so helpful. Poor thing. How terrible to lose her mother like that, and so young."

He shook his head. "I have no idea how such a dreadful woman managed to raise such a beautiful daughter." He didn't say it with anger but merely as though it were a well-known fact. Naturally, I asked the obvious, nosy question. "How do you know Amelia?"

"She is a friend of my son."

The way he said friend suggested perhaps the relationship was warmer. "Friend? Or girlfriend?"

He chuckled. "Lucy, you ask questions like an American."

"I am an American." I looked at him sideways, hoping he found this charming and not irritating. "So?"

"So, my son worked at an Indian restaurant as a busboy. It is near the ladies' college, and the girls often go there for a meal when they are sick of that institutional food they get. She became friendly with my son, and one thing led to another."

"That's nice. It must be very hard to meet boys when you go to an all-girls' school."

"My wife and I did not entirely approve of the relationship. Our son must work very hard to get into medical school. We like him to have a job because it's important to develop a good work ethic. But he didn't have time for a girlfriend. However, Amelia is a lovely young woman, not silly and flighty like some of those girls. She also takes her future seriously." He sighed. "We did not know she was keeping this friendship a secret from her parents. Somehow her mother found out. She showed up at the restaurant where my son worked. Made a terrible scene. Humiliated him in public. Said she would have him arrested if he went near her daughter again."

I could picture the scene, and my whole body was filled with the horror of what it must've been like.

He had to take a breath before he could go on. "Fortunately, the people who own the restaurant are old friends, and they know Ashvin. They know he is a good boy. But still, many of the regular patrons heard her. He wasn't fired, but he left the job. Said he couldn't go back." He shook his head. "That woman didn't know anything about him, and she said such things."

I didn't know what to say. "I am so sorry." Amelia did look like a nice girl. And I could imagine Vinod's son being like him. Serious and honorable.

"Well, from what Amelia said earlier, she obviously felt terrible but too frightened of her mother to make a stand."

It was obvious that Vinod thought the world of his son. He might talk about the incident in a calm way, but I doubted he had been calm at the time. In fact, he must have been furious. And then, to come on this knitting show and discover the woman who'd humiliated his beloved son and caused his young heart to be broken was here, boasting about her high hopes for her own beloved daughter—perhaps he snapped.

I was suddenly glad that it was a sunny afternoon and there were plenty of people around.

CHAPTER 19

*D*uring lunch, I tried to work out whether Vinod could be a murderer, then decided that he couldn't. He just seemed too nice. Then I looked around the rest of the table, but none of them seemed the type. However, I should've known by now that there really wasn't a type of murderer. People were driven to crazy acts. Maybe they'd been crazy all along and hid it well.

I ordered a salad with goat cheese for lunch, though I was barely hungry after William's breakfast this morning of blueberry pancakes with real Vermont maple syrup that had made me momentarily homesick. William had said, "Lucy, it's a pleasure to watch you eat."

"Make a pig of myself, you mean. Please join me. You know Rafe won't."

It didn't take too much persuading to get William to join me for pancakes. As we sat over a second cup of coffee, I asked him why he stayed. "You obviously miss cooking, and you're so good at it. You should open a restaurant or go into wedding catering or something."

He shook his head. "I'd never leave Rafe."

"But why? I'm sure he pays well and he's, well, amazing, but your talents are wasted here."

He looked into his coffee. I stayed quiet until at last he spoke. "My family have been serving Rafe for hundreds of years."

I leaned forward, and I was sure there was a stupid expression on my face. "Come again?"

He grinned at me. "I know. It sounds mad, but it's true. My many times great-grandfather owed Rafe his life, or so the legend goes. He promised that his son and all his son's sons would look after his master after he was gone." He shrugged. "And we always have."

This sounded like feudal times. "And none of you ever said, 'You know, you're a great guy, Rafe, but I'd rather be a cobbler or join the circus or try out for astronaut school?'"

"No. Never. Each of us teaches our eldest son how to serve Rafe, and when he's old enough, he takes over and we retire." He leaned forward, and his eyes were intent. "Loyalty, duty and honor. They aren't concepts that are as revered now as they used to be, but we Threshers would give our lives for Rafe. It's who we are."

I felt out of my depth here. Somehow, I thought he'd been brainwashed by his father, who'd been brainwashed by his and so on back down the line. "But you're stuck out here in this admittedly beautiful manor house. You could have your own restaurant in London or New York. You are that good." Okay, I wasn't the world's preeminent food critic, but I read those magazines on the plane that were always showcasing the latest, greatest new chef. William was easily as good as any chef or new restaurant I'd read about or even visited.

He shook his head. "I like it here. Maybe it's bred in my bones and marrow, but I wouldn't leave Rafe. I'm his until death."

"And I thank you for your loyalty, William." Rafe strolled in, dapper in a navy summer suit. "Ready, Lucy?"

William didn't turn a hair at our conversation being overheard, but I jumped up, feeling the blood rush to my face. "Yes. I just have to brush my teeth. I'll meet you at the car."

"No hurry."

I made horrible faces at myself in the mirror as I brushed my teeth. When was I going to learn to stay out of things that weren't my business?

I received a text during lunch, and to my surprise, it was from Ian. We used to text each other a lot, during that brief time we dated each other, but I'd assumed he'd deleted my number. Turned out he hadn't. The text said, "I know you're closed, but my auntie has run short of wool. Any chance I could stop by later and pick some up?"

I thought that was sweet that he was such a devoted great-nephew. Also, I had no problem with him coming to my shop out of hours. If I did him a professional favor, he might give me some information and perhaps share some of his initial findings in Enid Selfe's murder.

I texted back, "No problem. Come at seven." We were scheduled to shoot until six, and I wanted to be certain everyone was gone before Ian arrived.

Shortly after that, I received a text from Rafe. "Pick you up at ten PM."

I texted back that that was fine and enjoyed the fact that I was going to be the recipient of two gentleman callers this evening. One mortal and one not.

When Ian arrived, I had the wool all ready for him. I'd followed Gran's tradition of keeping files on all my customers, so I knew what they'd ordered. Of course, my files were all on computer. He looked a bit sheepish. "That's very kind of you, Lucy."

After he'd paid and I'd put the wool into a bag for him, he said, "I'm afraid I told you a bit of a porkie pie."

"You lied to me? What?"

"It was a white lie, really. My auntie asked me to pick up some more of this wool, but she didn't need it today. I wanted to talk to you."

He looked tired. He was wearing the suit he wore to work, and I suspected he'd been in it for a lot of hours. "You've been spending time with a lot of people who knew Enid Selfe. You have good instincts." He held up his hands in a helpless gesture, and the paper bag rustled. "Honestly, we're not getting anywhere. I'm asking for your help."

I was flattered that he wanted my input. It was smart of him because he was right. I was spending a lot of time with some of the last people to see Enid Selfe alive. "Of course. I'll tell you whatever I can. And in return, perhaps you'll tell me a few things."

He looked slightly offended. "That's not how it usually works."

"I know. But, as you said, this is a strange case. And I'm pretty heavily involved in it."

He looked to the space where the collection of antique knitting needles had hung and no longer did. I'd taken the entire display down and hidden it in the back room. It would be a long time before I could look at those antique knitting and crochet items without feeling sick. Molly had found me a nice poster of Teddy posing with his new book to put in its place.

Ian said, "All right. I can't tell you everything, but if you give me your word to keep anything I tell you quiet, I'll answer some questions." I nodded. He'd said to keep it quiet, not that I couldn't tell anyone. I felt that was enough permission that I could share whatever I learned with Theodore and Rafe.

"Well?" I asked. "What do you want to know?"

He let out a huge sigh. "Anything. Anything you can tell me

that might steer us in the right direction would be very helpful."

I felt sorry for Ian. It must be so difficult to try to find the one single person who might have murdered someone so very unpleasant. "You've taken a look at the three husbands, I assume?"

"Yes, yes," he said, rather testily. "What I want to know from you is more about the students in this class. Even the tech people behind the cameras. What do you know about them? You sit around all day knitting. Does anyone seem suspicious?"

"I'd start by taking a look at Gunnar."

He pulled out a notebook, and folded into it was a copy of the class list, slightly the worse for wear. "Gunnar is the Norwegian. Used to work on an oil rig." He glanced up at me. "It's funny you should mention him first. We're having trouble finding out about his background. The Norwegian authorities are saying they can't find him."

"I know this sounds crazy, but I'm not sure he's Norwegian at all. He swears in Danish."

Ian's eyes opened wide at that. "He swears in Danish?" He shrugged his shoulders up and down once. "Sometimes I swear in German." He thought about that. "In German, a curse sounds more like you mean it."

While I thought he had a point, I said, "Okay, this will sound even more stupid, but he looked confused when someone mentioned Preikestolen."

Now I really had Ian's interest. "Pulpit Rock?"

"You see. Even you've heard of it. And you're not Norwegian."

"No. That is odd. Of course, if we could fingerprint him, we might find out who he is, but there isn't enough reason to." He stared at the class list. "What else do you know about Gunnar?"

"Almost nothing. He listens more than he speaks. Maybe

that's why I noticed it when he would fumble a stitch and then swear. It was unusual to hear his voice."

"Right. Anything else?"

"He said he wouldn't have agreed to go on this program if he'd had any idea a woman would be murdered, but I expect we all feel that way."

I didn't know how much to tell. I didn't want to get nice people in trouble with the police. On the other hand, we did have a dead woman to find justice for. "I'm just throwing out some things for you. I have no idea if any of this is relevant, but Ryan was adopted. He told us all in class the first day. Enid Selfe said she gave up a child about his age. She joked that she could be his mother. Like it meant nothing to her. He never tried to find his birth mother, and she never tried to find her son. He said that if she turned out to be his mother he'd have to kill either himself or her. He said it in a sarcastic way, so I know it's a stretch, but I think it's worth checking out."

I could tell he thought it was a stretch, too. "All right. I'm willing to grasp at straws here. I'll look into it."

"While you're grasping, Annabel's family originally came from Jamaica. And Ryan has a Jamaican grandmother. Enid's second husband was with the immigration department. When his name was mentioned, I got the feeling that Annabel had heard his name before."

"More straws," he said, but he made a note in his notebook.

He was right. I had enough straws to weave a basket. "And today, Enid's daughter came to the shop."

He didn't look surprised at that. "The older one? Amelia?"

"That's right."

"She wanted to know everything she could about her mother's death. We told her the basics. I'm not really surprised that she came here. Awkward for you, though."

"No. I'd have wanted to come here, too, if I was her. Besides, we think Enid might have been like the evil stepmother in

Cinderella. The mother of the horrible stepsisters. She's awful to Cinderella but dotes on her own girls. Maybe Enid Selfe was like that. Horrible to most people, but her girls were everything to her. Amelia seemed devastated to have lost her."

He nodded. "I noticed that too. Well, anyone would be devastated to lose their mother like that, but she did seem as though she genuinely loved her."

"Poor girl."

"I'm glad you were kind to her."

"Not only me." And then I told him how surprised I had been that Vinod and she knew each other. "Now here's the interesting thing. She knew Vinod through his son."

"But doesn't she go to some posh girls' school?"

"Yes, she does. It's a boarding school. Vinod's son was working in a local Indian restaurant where the girls would sometimes go for a meal. I don't know how close they were, but it sounds as though Enid found out her daughter was dating a busboy and had a fit." I felt really uncomfortable casting suspicion on Vinod because I thought he was a very nice man, but very nice people could be driven to murder, especially to protect people they loved. "When Vinod talks about his son, his whole face lights up. He's that proud. And he seems like a genuinely devoted father. One who'd do anything for his son."

Ian caught the slight emphasis I'd put on *anything* and said, "Including murder?"

"I don't know. I'm just telling you everything I've observed. Do I think Vinod's a murderer? No. But I don't think any of them are."

"Speaking of people who'd do anything for the people they love, what about Douglas? Teddy's partner?"

I shook my head. "Him, I don't know. I haven't spent that much time with him, but he's definitely someone who would do anything for Teddy." I looked at the spot where Enid had died. "But as annoying and obstructive as Enid was, I bet Teddy and the filmmakers would've found a way to recut the footage so it wouldn't seem as bad as it was. Why murder her?"

He nodded. "I don't know much about how they make television shows, but I imagine you're right." He made another note. "I'll check with Molly."

He ran down the list of names. "What about Helen Radcliffe? Know much about her?"

"She's a science teacher, a beautiful knitter, seems to be enjoying the class. She and Enid didn't have much to do with each other."

He tapped his pen against his notebook. "And then there's the new woman."

"Margot Dodeson. Yes. She's certainly thrilled to be here and hangs on Teddy's every word. But I don't think she'd murder a woman just to get a spot in Teddy's class."

"Seems unlikely."

"And then there's all the crew," I reminded him, not wanting suspicion to fall only on the knitters.

"Found out anything interesting about them?"

"No. Only that Molly's under a lot of pressure to bring this in on time and on budget."

He looked at me seriously. "This is one of those things that you keep to yourself, but the rumor is that she's skating on thin ice. She was involved in a disastrous production that cost a lot and never got made. One more failure, and she'll be out of a job."

"Wow. She seems so confident, but I bet TV is the kind of industry that once your name is blackened, it's really hard to find another job."

"And Enid Selfe was putting this whole production in jeopardy. It's another straw."

"But is it the one that broke the camel's back?"

CHAPTER 20

$\mathcal{I}$an left, but I couldn't get that phrase out of my head. The straw that broke the camel's back. That one tiny thing that, after a load of other things, finally makes a person crack.

I had an idea. It was like the moment when all the different colored yarns came together in a pattern. If I was right, I knew who'd killed Enid Selfe.

I glanced at my watch and, making sure Ian was all the way gone, went into the back room. Swiftly and furtively, I pulled up the trapdoor and climbed down into the tunnel. Rafe hated me coming down here alone, but I didn't have far to go. I made my way quickly to the vampires' lair and knocked the special knock.

Gran and Sylvia were all dressed up and ready to go out. "Thank goodness I caught you," I said.

Gran hugged me. "How lovely to see you, dear. But whatever is the matter?"

I shook my head. "Nothing. But I want you to look at this list and tell me if you recognize any of the names on it."

She looked puzzled. "All right. Is this some kind of quiz?"

Alfred was sitting in the living room, but, of course, he heard every word. "I love quizzes. I'm very good at pub quizzes. Especially anything to do with history." He chuckled. "Well, I've lived quite a bit of it."

"I like a quiz, too," Sylvia added.

Gran shook her head. "You can't touch her on movies and theater."

Cold horror gripped my chest. "Gran, you're not going to pub quizzes, are you?"

She waved a hand in front of her face. "Not in Oxford, dear. But in Dublin. No one knows me in Dublin. It's such a pleasure to get out among people."

And Sylvia and Rafe were working to get her there. All that stood between her and the weekly pub quiz in Temple Bar was me and my selfish desire to keep her here.

She couldn't come to much harm in Dublin. The chances that one of her customers from Cardinal Woolsey's in Oxford would end up in a pub quiz in Dublin were extremely slim. And I thought it was far enough away that she could brazen it out and pretend to be someone else if that ghastly possibility ever became a reality. Anyone would believe they'd seen someone who looked like Gran rather than jump to the conclusion that my beloved grandmother was undead. At least I hoped they would.

We'd talk about her moving to Dublin, and soon, but right now, I had other things on my mind.

"This isn't a quiz. You knew most of your customers by name, didn't you?"

She looked quite indignant. "Not most of them. All of the regulars. And I hope you do, too. Individual customer service is what sets us apart from any old wool merchant you can find on the Internet."

I had heard this argument before. I assured her that as much as I was able, I was following in her footsteps with customer service. Or at least I was trying. I handed her the paper, and she ran her gaze down the page. It was still strange to see her without her glasses. But, of course, she didn't need them anymore.

She nodded and pointed to a name. "That one, of course. An excellent customer and an excellent knitter."

I pointed to another name. "What about that one?"

She shook her head. "No."

I went over to the super-powerful computer that sat on a priceless regency desk in the corner. I pulled up the file of class participants, including photographs, and showed Gran.

"Oh, yes, of course, I know that one." As she said the name, suddenly all those straws made themselves into a basket to catch a killer.

WE WERE GATHERED TOGETHER for the last time, those of us who were taking part in Teddy Lamont's lace class for Larch Wools. We were more subdued than we might have been. Enid Selfe's death hung heavy over us.

Margot Dodeson had stayed up most of the night, she said, to finish her cushion cover. It was beautiful. I wasn't sure if it was meant to be abstract, but it looked like a sunrise to me. From indigo to fuchsia, her colors blended and announced a beautiful day, a new beginning.

Everyone clapped. She was a much more pleasant class participant than her predecessor. She was quiet, eager to please and easily pleased herself. Teddy had taken quite a shine to her. It was ironic; Enid had hoped to be the class pet by virtue of her superb knitting skills, while her replacement, the mild and meek Margot, had become the class pet by being the opposite of her. Margot was an excellent knitter, but she was humble about it and obviously felt that it was a much higher talent to be good with color and design than to execute perfect stitches. Since Teddy absolutely agreed with her, they got on well.

In spite of the trauma and the setbacks, all of us had managed to finish our cushion covers. Mine was never going to win any awards, and due to my inept skills, it didn't look enough like a pentagram that anyone would point to it and scream *witch*. This was a good thing. And yet, I knew what I'd created. I planned to display it on the couch upstairs in my living room, a reminder of my heritage. Like most witches, my cushion would be hiding in plain sight.

I'd called and left a message with Ian, but he didn't call back until we were about to break for coffee. I excused myself and stepped outside to take the call.

"Ian, I think I know who did it," I said, trying to whisper but still be heard as a cyclist rode by singing opera. Only in Oxford.

"Well done, Lucy. Yes, we've got there too. Don't let anyone leave. I'm on my way."

"Okay." I would have liked to share my information, but it seemed I didn't need to.

We only had time for a quick coffee break at Elderflower before Molly was hurrying us all back. "We need to get all our filming finished today. The budget can't extend to overtime. Come on."

Teddy was in the highest of spirits and, even though my heart was heavy with dread, even I managed to smile and laugh at his antics.

All the cushion covers were beautiful and as individual as the knitters. Helen received so much praise, Teddy made her a star alongside Margot as he talked about their finished pieces on camera using words like "imaginative" and "daring."

The lace would be backed by silk, and he suggested much brighter colors than Helen had planned. But, for Helen, I thought this class had been a genuine breakthrough. She hadn't exactly colored outside the lines. She'd done an electron shell configuration of the elements, but her circles were precise. However, it was gorgeous and vivid. Teddy said to her, "How does it feel? To put some color in your world?"

"I'm quite pleased with it. I'm really very pleased." She sounded relieved, too, that taking chances had paid off. He patted her shoulder in today's muskrat-colored cardigan. "Helen, promise me that you will start knitting some of your sweaters in color. I want to see you bold and beautiful."

She ducked her head, looking shy. "I'll try."

There was a knock at my front door. Molly looked annoyed and went to answer it. There was a huge sign saying the shop was closed due to filming and please not to knock. However, when she saw who was doing the knocking, she opened the door. In came Ian Chisholm with two uniformed officers. *Two uniformed officers?* This looked serious.

My heart began to thump.

Teddy went straight up to them. Molly made cutting motions to the cameraman and the sound guy. Teddy said, "Detective Inspector Chisholm. Please tell me you have my phone. My life is on that thing."

"We'll get it back to you as soon as we can, sir."

Teddy looked at us and opened his arms wide. "If he doesn't have my phone, then why is he here?"

We all looked at Ian. He said, "We need everyone's help. Enid Selfe's murder has been a particularly difficult case to solve."

Annabel turned to Ryan. "Does that mean they know who did it?"

"How should I know?" He wasn't being as friendly with her as he had before she'd suggested he might have killed Enid.

Ian continued, "Enid Selfe was not a popular woman, and yet, she married three times. She was a beautiful knitter but managed to make enemies of everyone in this class."

I thought that was a bit brutal, but I wasn't about to argue with the detective who seemed to be going somewhere with this line of argument.

"Normally, in a murder investigation, the first thing we do is discard the leads that don't go anywhere. But, in this case, every one of the leads has directed us to a possible murderer."

Someone gasped. I wasn't sure if it was Annabel or Helen.

"Gunnar."

Gunnar started to rise, then, seeing three police officers between him and the door, sat down again. He looked like a caged wild animal. "Me? But I didn't even know the woman."

"You didn't know Gunnar Amundsen, either, when you assumed his identity."

There was another collective gasp, and this time more of us joined in.

"Your real name is Sven Henningsen, and you're not Norwegian at all, but Danish."

Gunnar went very red in the face, or I guess Sven did the blushing. He stood up as though he were going to leave. But, of course, there were still police at the door. He said, "I have paid for my crimes."

Ian continued as though he hadn't spoken. "You weren't in the North Sea when you learned to knit, were you? You learned to knit in prison."

"You have no right."

"Oh, I have every right." Ian glanced around the table. "Tell your fellow knitters what you were imprisoned for."

The Dane sat back down, looking defeated. "I killed a woman. But it was an accident."

"According to the evidence at your hearing, you killed a woman in a jealous rage."

"You don't know what it was like. You weren't there. We fought all the time. I pushed her. I shouldn't have done it, but I pushed her, and she tripped and hit her head. I didn't mean to kill her."

"That's not what the prosecution thought."

"I have done my time. I only want to live quietly and put the past behind me. That is why I changed my name."

"But your past followed you. Enid Selfe flirted with you at the book signing. Several people commented on it."

Really? I'd only noticed her with Rafe. Which showed where my interests lay.

Ian continued, "She made you think she was interested, and then she went cold. Moved on to other men. You sent her a message from Teddy's phone, knowing that she would come and meet him. Did she reject your advances? Is that why you killed her? Did she also trip and have an accident?"

The man we knew as Gunnar shook his head. "This is a fairytale. You have no proof."

"So this is the killer?" Vinod asked, staring at Gunnar.

"Not so fast," Ian replied. "You kept some things from us too. Didn't you?"

Vinod looked at the detective with dignity. "I answered all your questions."

"You said you hadn't known Enid Selfe before you met her here in Oxford," Ian said. He reached for his notebook. "Shall I read you back your own words?"

Vinod shook his head. "What I said was true. I never met that woman. For the rest, it was not my story to tell."

"Fathers. Mothers. Beloved children. That's a story that's played out here." I felt bad that I had been the one to start Ian down the path where Vinod, his son, Enid Selfe's daughter and Enid herself converged. But I had thought it might be important, and clearly Ian thought so too. He said, "Your son and Enid's daughter, Amelia, were more than friends, weren't they? They believed themselves in love. And Enid put a stop to that. She humiliated your son in public, broke his heart and nearly got him fired from his job." He stared at Vinod. "You're a proud father. You must have been mad enough to kill."

Vinod gave a tiny smile. "Enid Selfe was not the only one who disapproved of the match," he said. "Amelia is a very nice girl, but I don't believe my son should be spending so much time with the young woman. He needs to focus on his studies."

"And yet, from everything I can tell, the two of them are back together again now that her mother is dead."

Vinod looked genuinely shocked. "That young woman needs a friend. Yes, we have welcomed her back into our family. I've told her she can come over any time that she needs a place to go or a good meal. I'm fond of her. We all are. It doesn't mean I want my son to marry her. They are only seventeen."

Annabel spoke up. "Vinod couldn't have done it. We're staying at the same hotel. The night of the murder, I couldn't sleep. It was hot. Around midnight, I got up to open my window, and when I looked out, I saw Vinod sitting outside, smoking a cigarette."

Vinod shook his head. "It is a terrible habit. I am ashamed that you should see me, but I felt quite perturbed having learned that Enid Selfe was in our knitting class. I wasn't certain I could continue."

Smoking might be dangerous to his health, but it looked like the cancer sticks had saved his butt in this case.

Ian wasn't buying it though. "Annabel. How convenient that you should give Vinod an alibi. It naturally gives you one as well."

CHAPTER 21

*A*nnabel opened her eyes wide. "Me? Why do I need an alibi?" She glanced around. "What are you planning to do? Arrest everybody?"

He flipped through his notes and stopped when he found the place he wanted. "Does the name Horace Crisfield mean anything to you?"

Her hands clenched involuntarily, scrunching her beautiful lacework. "What about him? He's dead, and good riddance to him."

"As I said, the more we searched each of your backgrounds, the more links we found to Enid Selfe, or in this case, one of her husbands."

"Horace Crisfield was a horrible man. I don't care who knows it. He deported my granddad back to Jamaica. Granddad hadn't seen Jamaica since he was two years old. I hired the best lawyer I could afford. Oh, we got him back. But he had a heart attack from the stress. He's never been the same since."

"I'm so sorry," Ryan said, putting his hand over hers. She turned hers over and gripped his fingers.

Ian said, "Horace Crisfield was dead. But then Enid Selfe

announced to you that he'd done the right thing. Don't bother
to deny it. Several people overheard the conversation. Perhaps
you decided you'd found the perfect revenge. If you couldn't
hurt Crisfield, you could punish Enid Selfe."

"Nonsense. What Crisfield and his cronies did was wrong.
Terribly, terribly wrong. But how would it help my granddad if
I became a murderer? No. I loathed Enid Selfe, her racism, and
everything she stood for. I won't pretend I'm sorry she's dead,
but I didn't kill her."

Helen was watching the two of them. She said, "No offense,
but if anyone had a motive, it was Ryan."

Ryan turned to her. "What?"

"You are the one that said if she turned out to be your
mother, you'd have to kill her."

His jaw dropped. "I was only joking. Anyway, she wasn't my
mother." He turned to Ian. "Was she?"

Ian said, "You'd have to have DNA testing to be certain. You
might want to do that to ease your mind."

Ryan let out a breath. "So you don't suspect me?"

"Oh, I do. I suspect all of you. And until someone remem-
bers something or admits to the crime, we're going to sit here,
and I will sift through all the evidence." He glared around
fiercely at us. "One of you knows something. Or you saw
something."

Teddy suddenly spoke up. "Well, I didn't. That woman was
nothing to me. I'm bored of all this drama. I've a knitting class
to teach, and I'd like to get on with it. And I want my phone
back by the end of the day, or you'll hear from my lawyers."

Ian said, "Mr. Lamont, you've as much reason as anyone to
want that woman dead. She ruined your first day of filming.
She was going to ruin the entire televised class. Your brand is
all about the way you connect with your fans."

Gunnar spoke up for the first time. "And it was your cell
phone that sent the text. Perhaps you sent it yourself."

"Well, I didn't. Molly, tell them. You'd already promised to find me a replacement. I went all diva on her ass until she agreed. I didn't have to kill Enid Selfe. I just had to tell the staff to make a change."

Molly walked over to stand beside Teddy. She looked tired and stressed. "He's right. It was my responsibility."

"It's always your responsibility, isn't it? Word is, this isn't your first disaster. One more, and you were out in a very unforgiving industry. You needed this show to go well."

She rubbed her eyes. "Yes. I did, and I do. But I didn't have to murder a woman to get this show back on track. All I had to do was replace her."

"We're not getting anywhere," Annabel said. "You've now accused everybody but Lucy and Helen of being the murderer."

Ian smiled the kind of smile that made me nervous. It seemed to have the same effect on Helen. "Yes. Now we come to Helen."

She glanced up nervously. "Yes?"

"She didn't even recognize you, did she?"

Helen tried to look innocent, but I could see her shoulders climbing up around her ears. "Who?"

"Enid Selfe. The woman who gave you a nervous breakdown so you left the job you'd loved for eight years."

Vinod's eyes widened. "Of course. Why did I not put two and two together? You taught at Castle Bromwich Ladies' College. The school Amelia attends."

"That's right. I did." Her hands were shaking so badly, she clasped them together and put them in her lap.

Ian pulled a photograph from a file and handed it to Vinod. Naturally, I leaned over for a peek. I had never seen such a transformation in my life. The woman in the photograph had shoulder-length dark hair. She wore a smart suit, stylish eyeglasses, and her face looked firm and confident. The woman in the photo was Helen, but she'd lost all of her color and aged a couple of decades since that photograph.

We all glanced at Ian, who said, "That picture was taken at a staff event only three years ago, wasn't it, Helen?"

She glanced at the photo and nodded. "Enid Selfe destroyed my career, my happiness, my health and nearly destroyed me."

"You must have hated her."

She nodded. "I think the worst of it was that her daughter's a genuinely nice young woman. Clever, but not brilliant. She'll do well at a second-tier university, but that woman had an obsession about getting that girl into Oxford or Cambridge. She became convinced that I wasn't doing enough, that I wasn't qualified. She reported me to the headmistress on several occasions. Wanted me replaced. She'd accuse me of sloppy teaching any time her daughter didn't get top marks. It's amazing how destructive one person can be. She even got other parents to side with her. She destroyed my peace, she destroyed my confidence, and finally, she destroyed my health."

In a conversational tone, Ian said, "We found a partial fingerprint on one of the knitting needles that was driven into Enid Selfe's chest. It was yours."

Her head jerked up. "What? That's impossible."

"Why? Because you wiped them so carefully? You missed a spot."

She shook her head. "No." She glanced at me wildly. "Lucy, you remember. That first day. I was admiring the display of needles. I must've touched one."

I didn't remember that at all. I shook my head, feeling sorry for her.

Ian said, "Helen Radcliffe, I'll need you to come down to the station to help us with our inquiries."

"I can't... I didn't... I need to call my husband."

He nodded. "When we get to the station."

"At least let me get my pills."

Margot Dodeson rose and collected her bag. "Well, I'm obviously in the way." She smiled at Teddy. "Thank you very much for the excellent class. It's been an honor."

I watched Margot walk away, not taking the most direct path to the door, but walking in a curve. I said, "Margot? Why wouldn't you walk straight to the door?"

She turned, looking startled, as did everyone around the table. "I beg your pardon?"

I stood up for the first time. I'd been quiet until now. Like Ian, I had seen too many suspects and no obvious murderer. Until last night.

"Every time you walk in or out of this shop, you go around the spot where Enid Selfe was killed. But how would you know that? Unless you'd been there."

Margot backed up until she bumped the wall of wools. She looked so timid, you'd think a mouse would scare her away. "Lucy, I really believe the stress is getting to you, dear."

"When did you go back to your maiden name?"

Two bright spots of color appeared in her pale cheeks. "It was a personal choice after my divorce. Many women do."

It was Gran who had remembered her married name, but obviously I couldn't give my undead grandmother any sleuthing credit, so I said, "I was confused. You seemed like a recent customer, but you spoke of knowing my Gran and things that happened years ago. When I looked back in the files, I found a Margot Vincent. That was you."

"It's not a crime to change your name. I must go now. It's been lovely."

She took another step toward the door, but this time, Ian stopped her. "Vincent?"

He turned to me, looking puzzled. "That wasn't one of the husbands, was it?"

"No. It was one of the boyfriends. Enid Selfe was not a nice woman. She seemed to need every man she met to fall in love with her. It was kind of an obsession with her, wasn't it?" I asked Margot.

"I've no idea," she said primly.

"Your husband wasn't rich or titled. He was simply unavailable. He was a married building contractor who worked on Enid's home. While he was working there, they began an affair."

Margot put her hands over her face. "No," she said in a strangled voice. I felt sorry for her, but the truth had to come out.

"Maybe she was bored. Maybe she thought she'd get a better price if they were lovers. Maybe she just wanted whatever she couldn't have. Who knows why she went after your husband? But she did, and he left you, planning to marry her." I made myself deliberately cruel. "He dumped you, his boring but faithful wife of what? Twenty years? And ran off with Enid. Just up and left, after all you'd done for him."

"I wouldn't do something like that." But her voice was wavering.

"You still wear your wedding ring. That's why I didn't realize you were divorced. I bet you hang on to all sorts of things from the past. I bet if the police got a warrant to search your home they'd find something heavy. Something that had meaning for you." I was making this story up as I went along but Margot was becoming increasingly agitated so I thought maybe I was close to the truth. "One of the tools your husband left behind, perhaps? Something heavy, like a hammer that he could have used in Enid Selfe's home renovation. You wouldn't have thrown the murder weapon away. You'd have kept it. As a reminder. She took everything from you, but you got your revenge, in the end. The police will find traces, you know, of her blood. That's what will convict you."

Suddenly she dropped her hands and faced me fiercely. "He

was all I had. He was my life. I wasn't only his wife. I did the books for the business. We were a team. And she took him away. And then, when he wanted to marry her, she said no. She took him away from me, and she didn't even want him." Her voice was rising now. "I'd have taken him back. I would. But she'd done something to him. He didn't want me anymore, even though he couldn't have her." She wailed. "She took everything from me, and she didn't even want him."

I glanced over at Ian to see if he wanted to take over, but he motioned me to continue. "When you came into my shop the other day, you didn't know she'd be here, did you?"

I remembered now how overwrought Margot had been. I'd assumed she was starstruck by Teddy. But that wasn't what affected her. She'd recognized Enid Selfe, the woman who'd destroyed her marriage and probably her life.

"No. It was a terrible shock to see her there. And I watched her pawing at Teddy. And then at that book signing, fluttering around every man there. She was like vermin. She had to be destroyed."

"How did you get the key to get into my shop?"

"They were lying about everywhere. Neatly labeled too. I took the cameraman's key."

The burly cameraman said sheepishly, "So that's where the key went. Blimey, I thought I'd lost it."

The glance Molly sent him suggested there would be retribution later for his carelessness in not reporting the key missing. I saw Becks make a note.

I continued, "And then you followed Teddy, waiting for your chance to steal his phone."

She shook her head. "No. I was going to slip a note under Enid's door at the hotel. That was going to be the most difficult part, getting her to believe Teddy had written the note and then making sure I got it back again so no one would suspect me." She seemed relieved now that she was talking. "But when I got to the hotel, Teddy was there. In the bar, having a beer." She glanced over at him. "You didn't even notice me there. I watched until you went to the toilet, and then it was easy enough to slip your phone out of your pocket."

Teddy looked very disappointed in Margot. "I trusted you. You were my star."

"I'm sorry. I sent the text and put the phone back in your pocket before you even returned. No one noticed. No one ever does notice me."

Ian formally arrested Margot Dodeson. As she was led away by a female officer, Gunnar said, "At least she knows how to knit. It will pass the time in prison."

Ryan let out a breath. "I don't know about the rest of you, but I need a drink. Let's go to the pub."

"Perhaps it is better if I do not come," Gunnar—no, Sven said.

Helen put her hand on his shoulder. "We all have parts of our past we'd redo if we could. Come on, Sven."

Once more, everyone headed for the pub. Minus Margot Dodeson.

CHAPTER 22

The film crew had cleared everything from my shop, and I was putting things back in order before opening in the morning. The fate of the TV show was in limbo. The producers needed to decide whether to go ahead, knowing the behind-the-scenes drama would draw viewers, or whether to cancel.

Teddy was all for going ahead, of course. He was firmly in the no publicity is bad publicity camp. Molly agreed with him, but it wouldn't be her decision.

I didn't really have an opinion. My shop was a normal knitting and yarn shop once more, and I was happy to have it that way. I liked Teddy, but I'd replaced the poster. Becks had come by with a thank you gift for me. They'd blown up one of the stills of Nyx curled up in her basket, surrounded by colorful wools, looking particularly adorable.

Nyx was happily snoozing in the front window, even now, in a similar pose.

The Oxford newspaper sat on the cash desk. The sensational murder and arrest were front page news. Margot wouldn't have a trial. She'd confessed to the crime and would be sentenced, soon. I'd been partly right about the murder weapon. She hadn't used one of her husband's tools to kill Enid, as he'd taken them all when he moved out.

Instead, she'd taken an ornamental stone frog from the garden. She'd told the police it had been the first gift her husband had given her when they'd moved into their home. After dispatching Enid Selfe, she'd returned the frog to its accustomed spot. Police had found traces of the murdered woman's blood on the frog.

Satisfied that all was in order, in my shop and in the small world of Harrington Street, I thought I'd walk up to the corner market to get something for dinner, now I was no longer staying with Rafe. I found I missed him, and I definitely missed William's cooking.

When I stepped outside, I felt something gritty under my feet. I looked down and saw a line of small crystals scattered across the threshold. I leaned down and picked up a pinch between my finger and thumb. It looked like sand, but I was fairly certain I'd seen this substance before. It was Dead Sea salt.

I went back inside and walked around the shop investigating, and sure enough, there were traces of salt all the way around the perimeter. I picked up my phone and immediately called Margaret Twigg before I could think better of it. "What did you do to my shop?"

"And hello to you, too, Lucy," she said in a condescending tone. "As I recall, what I did in your shop was relieve it of a lingering ghost."

"Not that. Why is there salt across my threshold and around all the edges of the shop?"

"You found it, did you? You're coming along."

I felt hot and irritable and uninterested in bandying words with Margaret Twigg. I didn't say anything, just waited. Finally she said, "Relax, Lucy. It's a protection spell. Lavinia asked me to do it, since her granddaughter works in Cardinal Woolsey's. When she discovered that a longtime customer was a murderer, well, who's to say there aren't more of them? Best to be on the safe side."

"But you used Dead Sea salt. I thought you used that to get rid of the spirits of the dead."

"Dead Sea salt is wonderful stuff. Multipurpose. You should get yourself some. You can buy it online."

I knew what she could do with her protection spell. As soon as I got her off the phone, I grabbed the wooden-handled wicker broom that stood in the corner and began sweeping the salt toward the door. I heard a shriek behind me and turned to find my grandmother standing there. "Lucy! What are you doing?"

I would have thought my action was self-evident. "Sweeping up."

"Be very careful, dear. You need a spell and the right intent, or you'll sweep out all the good energy instead of the bad."

"Are you kidding me? Can't a broom just be a broom?"

"Not when you're special."

Gran come toward me and took the broom out of my hands. "Lucy, dear. You are a witch, and that is a very ancient broom. It was mine and my mother's before me and hers before her." She didn't say any more, just looked at me with a penetrating gaze.

I looked at the broom and then at her. "You're not seriously trying to tell me that I could fly on that thing?"

"Well, not without a lot of practice. And certainly not with that attitude."

"Unbelievable." Every time I turned around, some other cliché was coming true. Witches cast spells and sprinkled salt across thresholds. I had a black cat who was a familiar. And now my grandmother was telling me I could fly on a broom?

I really needed to sit down.

"Why didn't you tell me this before?"

"These things come to us when we're ready. That broom will stay in the corner until you need it. Just be careful. I wouldn't use it for regular cleaning."

And she put it back in the corner. Nyx walked over to the corner and sniffed the broom, then looked at me like a dog ready to jump in the car and go for a ride.

"Oh, no," I said. "I'll tell you one thing. You are never getting me on one of those things."

Nyx stared at me with her golden eyes and did not look convinced.

I hope you enjoyed *Lace and Lies*. Read on for a sneak peek of *Bobbles and Broomsticks*, Vampire Knitting Club Book 8.

A Note from Nancy

Dear Reader,

Thank you for reading the Vampire Knitting Club series. I am so grateful for all the enthusiasm this series has received. I have plenty more stories about Lucy and her undead knitters planned for the future.

I hope you'll consider leaving a review and please tell your friends who like cozy mysteries.

Review on Amazon, Goodreads or BookBub.

Your support is the wool that helps me knit up these yarns. Turn the page for a sneak peek of *Bobbles and Broomsticks*, Book 8 of the Vampire Knitting Club.

I hope to see you in my private Facebook Group. It's a lot of fun. www.facebook.com/groups/NancyWarrenKnitwits

Until next time,
Happy Reading,

Nancy

BOBBLES AND BROOMSTICKS

CHAPTER 1

Moreton-under-Wychwood wasn't a famous town in England. You wouldn't find it on any Tripadvisor top ten list so it rarely enticed tourists. However, it was a very pretty little village in Oxfordshire with a beautiful and well kept village green, picturesque stone cottages, some with thatch roofs, and over-looking all, like a tired old sentry, was the church tower.

St. John the Divine church was originally Norman, built around 1200 according to local historians. Over time it had been patched up, propped up and bits of it rebuilt, but its heart was ancient. Walking in on a warm September day I felt the sudden chill as the stone walls surrounded me. I thought of coffins and stone mausoleums which made me shiver, thankful for the blue hand-knit cardigan my undead grandmother had made for me. I wore it over a blue and white linen dress and sandals.

Soon my momentary chill was dispelled as three giggling women entered behind me. First came Alice Robinson who worked at Frogg's Books across the road from Cardinal

Woolsey's, my wool and knitting shop. An excellent knitter, Alice sometimes taught knitting classes for me. Now she was marrying Charlie Wright, the owner of Frogg's Books. I was to be a bridesmaid at their upcoming wedding. She and Charlie were getting married in this very church and we were here to plan the decorations. Flower arrangements for the front of the church and pew bows were both allowed. With Alice was my cousin Violet who was a witch, like me, and Alice's friend from school, Beatrice.

After stopping at the church, we were heading to the bridal shop for our final dress fittings. Beatrice had an art degree and ideas about how the flowers should be. Alice was happy to let her make the decorating decisions which left me free to wander around the church. I tried to make out the names of people memorialized in stone on the church floor, but time and footsteps had all but obliterated the old ones. The pews were wooden and featured needlepointed cushions, faded with time, for the faithful to sit on.

I wandered around, my sandals scraping on the flagstones, peering at the stone font, the tattered war banners, the memorials set into the wall that were easier to read as no one had stepped on them. Here was one to Henry Herbert, landowner and his wife Ann who both died in 1678. I moved on to read the next one and felt the ground beneath me shift. Constance Crosyer 1538 to 1608, beloved wife of Sir Rafe Crosyer, 1528 to 1610. My heart began to thump and my breath came in quick gasps.

"Lucy?" It was Violet calling me and she sounded as though she were far away. "Lucy, what is it?" I breathed deep and schooled my face to calmness before turning. *Beloved wife of Rafe Crosyer.* What was wrong with me? In all these centuries of course Rafe had been married. Probably many times. *Beloved.* Would he one day use that word about me?

I walked back to where the three women stood now in front

of the altar. "This is where we'll stand," Alice explained. We already knew the order of bridesmaids. First me, then Vi, and then Beatrice who was maid of honor. Alice was a sensible, practical woman, but today she seemed filled with romance and whimsy. She glanced at us, her eyes dancing. "Shall we practice the walk up the aisle?"

"But there's a proper rehearsal tomorrow," I reminded her. I wanted to get out of this place where Constance would always be beloved and where Rafe had once pretended to be dead.

"Don't be a killjoy, Lucy," Violet chided me. I looked at the three happy faces, as eager as little girls to play brides and bridesmaids.

"Fine, of course," I said.

"Thank you. I feel so sure I'll trip over one of the flagstones," Alice admitted. "I want to keep practicing."

"You'll be fine," Violet said. I saw her lips move and knew she was casting a spell, making sure Alice's path was smooth as she walked up the aisle.

We took our places and Beatrice, who turned out to be a singer as well as an artist, began to sing, in a full, rich soprano, "Here comes the bride."

"Lucy, go," Violet ordered, "And remember to smile," as though she were the wedding planner. Still, I did as I was told. I pictured all the people in the pews and walked slowly up the aisle in time to the singing. I held an imaginary bouquet in front of me. When I reached the altar I stopped and turned. Violet was already on the move. She also held an imaginary bouquet and she smiled as though a photographer was going to capture the moment for the front page of a bridal magazine.

As she grew closer, I heard a sound above, like a creaking door. I looked up but all I saw was thick wooden beams stretching across and above supporting the stone roof. When she reached me, I said, "Did you hear that?"

"What? Lucy, you're as nervous as a mouse in a cattery."

"You didn't hear a creaking noise?"

"No. I heard Beatrice singing. Pull yourself together."

Before Beatrice reached us, walking up the aisle while still singing, I whispered, "On the wall over there is a memorial stone to Rafe's wife, Constance, and it mentioned Sir Rafe Crosyer's date of death. 1610."

She nodded. "What choice did he have? He couldn't stay here forever, not aging. Once his wife passed away, he left these parts. He was gone a very long time."

"He must have loved her very much."

Vi leaned in closer. "She was one of us."

"You mean?"

"Yes, Lucy. Rafe's first wife, Constance Crosyer was a witch."

I glanced up again. Maybe Constance was the one groaning, warning me to stay away from her husband.

Order your copy today! *Bobbles and Broomsticks* is Book 8 in the Vampire Knitting Club series.

ALSO BY NANCY WARREN

The best way to keep up with new releases, plus enjoy bonus content and prizes is to join Nancy's newsletter at NancyWarrenAuthor.com or join her in her private Facebook group Nancy Warren's Knitwits.

∽

Vampire Knitting Club: Paranormal Cozy Mystery

Tangles and Treasons - a free prequel for Nancy's newsletter subscribers

The Vampire Knitting Club - Book 1

Stitches and Witches - Book 2

Crochet and Cauldrons - Book 3

Stockings and Spells - Book 4

Purls and Potions - Book 5

Fair Isle and Fortunes - Book 6

Lace and Lies - Book 7

Bobbles and Broomsticks - Book 8

Popcorn and Poltergeists - Book 9

Garters and Gargoyles - Book 10

Diamonds and Daggers - Book 11

Herringbones and Hexes - Book 12

Ribbing and Runes - Book 13

Cat's Paws and Curses - A Holiday Whodunnit

Vampire Knitting Club Boxed Set: Books 1-3

Vampire Knitting Club Boxed Set: Books 4-6

The Great Witches Baking Show: Culinary Cozy Mystery

The Great Witches Baking Show - Book 1

Baker's Coven - Book 2

A Rolling Scone - Book 3

A Bundt Instrument - Book 4

Blood, Sweat and Tiers - Book 5

Crumbs and Misdemeanors - Book 6

A Cream of Passion - Book 7

Cakes and Pains - Book 8

Gingerdead House - A Holiday Whodunnit

The Great Witches Baking Show Boxed Set: Books 1-3

Vampire Book Club: Paranormal Women's Fiction Cozy Mystery

Crossing the Lines - Prequel

The Vampire Book Club - Book 1

Chapter and Curse - Book 2

A Spelling Mistake - Book 3

Toni Diamond Mysteries

Toni is a successful saleswoman for Lady Bianca Cosmetics in this series of humorous cozy mysteries.

Frosted Shadow - Book 1

Ultimate Concealer - Book 2

Midnight Shimmer - Book 3

A Diamond Choker For Christmas - A Holiday Whodunnit

The Almost Wives Club

An enchanted wedding dress is a matchmaker in this series of romantic comedies where five runaway brides find out who the best men really are!

The Almost Wives Club: Kate - Book 1

Second Hand Bride - Book 2

Bridesmaid for Hire - Book 3

The Wedding Flight - Book 4

If the Dress Fits - Book 5

Take a Chance series

Meet the Chance family, a cobbled together family of eleven kids who are all grown up and finding their ways in life and love.

Chance Encounter - Prequel

Kiss a Girl in the Rain - Book 1

Iris in Bloom - Book 2

Blueprint for a Kiss - Book 3

Every Rose - Book 4

Love to Go - Book 5

The Sheriff's Sweet Surrender - Book 6

The Daisy Game - Book 7

Take a Chance Box Set - Prequel and Books 1-3

Abigail Dixon Mysteries: 1920s Cozy Historical Mystery

In 1920s Paris everything is très chic, except murder.

Death of a Flapper - Book 1

For a complete list of books, check out Nancy's website at NancyWarrenAuthor.com

ABOUT THE AUTHOR

Nancy Warren is the USA Today Bestselling author of more than 70 novels. She's originally from Vancouver, Canada, though she tends to wander and has lived in England, Italy and California at various times. While living in Oxford she dreamed up The Vampire Knitting Club. Favorite moments include being the answer to a crossword puzzle clue in Canada's National Post newspaper, being featured on the front page of the New York Times when her book Speed Dating launched Harlequin's NASCAR series, and being nominated three times for Romance Writers of America's RITA award. She has an MA in Creative Writing from Bath Spa University. She's an avid hiker, loves chocolate and most of all, loves to hear from readers!

The best way to stay in touch is to sign up for Nancy's newsletter at NancyWarrenAuthor.com or join her private Facebook group facebook.com/groups/NancyWarrenKnitwits

To learn more about Nancy and her books
NancyWarrenAuthor.com

CPSIA information can be obtained
at www.ICGtesting.com
Printed in the USA
LVHW010453211221
706819LV00010B/604